THE EXTRA YARD

A
HOME TEAM
NOVEL

THE
EXTRA
YARD

MIKE
LUPICA

SIMON & SCHUSTER BOOKS FOR YOUNG READERS
NEW YORK LONDON TORONTO SYDNEY NEW DELHI

SIMON & SCHUSTER BOOKS FOR YOUNG READERS
An imprint of Simon & Schuster Children's Publishing Division
1230 Avenue of the Americas, New York, New York 10020
This book is a work of fiction. Any references to historical events, real people, or real places are used fictitiously. Other names, characters, places, and events are products of the author's imagination, and any resemblance to actual events or places or persons, living or dead, is entirely coincidental.
Text copyright © 2016 by Mike Lupica
Cover illustration copyright © 2016 by Dave Seeley
All rights reserved, including the right of reproduction in whole or in part in any form.
SIMON & SCHUSTER BOOKS FOR YOUNG READERS is a trademark of Simon & Schuster, Inc.
For information about special discounts for bulk purchases, please contact Simon & Schuster Special Sales at 1-866-506-1949 or business@simonandschuster.com.
The Simon & Schuster Speakers Bureau can bring authors to your live event. For more information or to book an event, contact the Simon & Schuster Speakers Bureau at 1-866-248-3049 or visit our website at www.simonspeakers.com.
Also available in a Simon & Schuster Books for Young Readers hardcover edition
Book design by Lucy Ruth Cummins
The text for this book was set in Adobe Garamond Pro.
Manufactured in the United States of America
0119 OFF
First Simon & Schuster Books for Young Readers paperback edition March 2017
4 6 8 10 9 7 5 3
The Library of Congress has cataloged the hardcover edition as follows:
Lupica, Mike.
The extra yard / Mike Lupica.
pages cm.— (Home team)
Summary: "Teddy has been training all summer with his new friends Jack and Gus to make the new travel football team in Walton, but when his long-absent dad comes back to town and into his life he is faced with a much bigger challenge"— Provided by publisher.
ISBN 978-1-4814-1000-7 (hc)
[1. Football—Fiction. 2. Fathers and sons—Fiction.] I. Title.
PZ7.L97914Fx 2016
[Fic]—dc23
2015013657
ISBN 978-1-4814-1001-4 (pbk)
ISBN 978-1-4814-1002-1 (eBook)

For the great Esther Newberg

THE EXTRA YARD

ONE

Teddy Madden felt better about himself than he ever had before. Even though he was scared out of his mind.

He was starting eighth grade next week, but he wasn't scared about starting another year in school. He was actually excited about that.

He was scared about football.

In two days he had tryouts for the Walton Wildcats, a new football team for the best kids his age, even though he had never played a game of organized football before.

He kept telling himself he was in the best shape of his life. In the past he'd joked that he had no shape, other than maybe a blob. He had a good attitude about sports for the first time. That was thanks to his friend Jack Callahan.

It was Jack who'd nominated himself last spring to become Teddy's personal trainer. Jack basically told Teddy he was going to get in shape or else.

Teddy hated the workouts at first. But slowly he came to like them, and then love them. Mostly he loved the way they made him feel good about himself. Before then, he just figured self-esteem was for somebody else's self. Not anymore. Teddy felt good, and not just about being in this kind of shape. He and Jack weren't just teammates. They were friends.

They were *boys*.

Teddy thought of himself as a whole new kid: Teddy Madden 2.0. So maybe it figured he would have new friends, too, like Jack and Gus Morales and Cassie Bennett. Cassie was the star of girls' sports in Walton the way Jack was for boys'.

Once Teddy started to get himself into shape, a lot of things began to happen, both in sports and in his life. For one thing, he ended up the catcher on the Walton baseball team, the Rays, which had made it all the way to the United States final of the Little League World Series in Williamsport, Pennsylvania.

Everybody on the team would always think they would have won the final if Jack had been able to pitch. But the Rays needed him in the semifinal, where he'd pitched a one-hitter in beating a team from Toledo. In the final the Rays fell behind 7–1. They came all the way back to tie, before losing in the bottom of the last inning to a pretty great team from Las Vegas.

Because of the way they had come back, though, they left Williamsport feeling as if they'd won something. Teddy was pretty sure that in Walton, people who'd watched their games on ESPN would always remember the near no-hitter Jack had pitched, and that big comeback against Las Vegas.

"The more you play," Jack said when they got home, "you find out there's more than one way to keep score in sports."

That baseball season had started with the old Teddy, the out-of-shape and overweight Teddy. He *was* a blob-shaped spectator. But he had ended up in Williamsport, hitting a two-run double to tie Vegas at 7–7. It was the kind of hit you always dreamed about hitting, in the big game, on national television. Teddy Madden had gotten that hit. Even if it wasn't enough to win that game for his team, he'd still gotten that hit.

By then, nobody was calling him by his old nickname: Teddy Bear.

On the baseball field behind Walton Middle School, one that Jack and Teddy were now using to play football, Jack said to Teddy, "We're going to need a new nickname for you."

It was just the two of them on a Thursday morning, the end of the last week before school. They threw Teddy's new football around on a field that was so close to his house it was almost like an extension of his backyard.

They took a quick break after going at it hard for an hour, sat on the grass, and drank Gatorade out of the bottles they'd brought. Teddy knew their rest period wouldn't last long. It never did with Jack Callahan.

"The one nickname I had before was more than enough," Teddy said. "You know how big my mom is on gluten-free food? My plan is to be nickname free."

Jack acted as if he hadn't even heard him. "How about Teddy the Tiger?"

"You make me sound like I should be telling you to eat your cereal," Teddy said. "And really? A tiger on a team called the Wildcats?"

"Excellent point," Jack said. He thought for a moment, frowning. "How about Terrible Ted?"

"Would I have to carry one of the Steelers' Terrible Towels?"

"This might turn out to be harder than I thought."

"You're not hearing me," Teddy said. "I don't want a

MIKE LUPICA

nickname. And by the way? You seem to be surviving without a nickname, except when Gus calls you Star."

"Which I hate."

"The way I hated Teddy Bear!" Teddy said. "It always made me feel like I was the class mascot, not just the class clown."

"I never thought you were either one," Jack said. "I always thought there was a warrior waiting to break out."

"A *warrior*?" Teddy said. "Are we getting ready to play football games, or video games? What do you think this is, Call of Duty?"

"Little bit," Jack said.

"Still don't know why you thought of me that way," Teddy said "A would-be warrior."

"I'm very observant," Jack said.

"So you can probably use those powers of observation to see how nervous I am about the day after tomorrow."

"You're going to make the team."

"You say."

"I know," Jack said.

"What if I start dropping passes all over the place?"

"You don't drop them when I throw them to you here, you're not going to drop them at Holzman."

Holzman Field was the field where the Wildcats would play their home games, in a brand-new elite league for their part of the country called All-American Football. The kids who didn't make the Wildcats would play on Walton's Pop Warner team.

"I wish I was as confident in me as you are," Teddy said. "But even if I don't make the Wildcats, at least I know I'll get to play Pop Warner."

Jack said, "You know that nickname you just said you hated? Let's not turn back into that guy now."

He casually reached over with his right fist. Teddy knuckle-bumped him.

"Okay?" Jack said.

"I'm still nervous."

"There's a good nervous in sports," Jack said. "I feel it all the time."

"You don't show it."

Jack laughed. "Clearly you're not as observant as I am."

"How do you tell the difference between nerves and choking?"

Jack shrugged. "No clue," he said. "Choking's not in my vocab. And it's not gonna be in yours."

As good as Jack was in sports, he was even better as a friend.

Teddy didn't care that Gus and Jack had been friends longer, or that Jack and Cassie were as close as a boy and girl could be without being boyfriend and girlfriend, at least not yet. When it came to Jack, Teddy just knew the most important thing you could know:

He could count on Jack.

And Jack knew he could count on Teddy.

Maybe it was because they'd been through so much together in a year. Teddy had been there for Jack when he'd briefly quit the baseball team, back when Jack was still blaming himself for the death of his older brother, Brad, in a dirt-bike accident, even though it wasn't Jack's fault at all.

But even while that was going on, and as much pain as Jack was in, it was Jack who stepped up one day at gym class and told the other guys to stop picking on Teddy because of his weight. Then he hadn't just helped Teddy to get into really good shape, he'd also helped Teddy find the confidence to face down his fears. And there were a lot of them at the time: fear of sports, fear of making friends, even a fear of heights.

Jack was also the first person Teddy had ever opened up to about his fear of being different from most of the kids he knew because he'd grown up without his dad around. His parents had divorced when Teddy was barely four years old, and his father moved all the way across the country to Oregon. Teddy saw him once a year, if that.

It was why Teddy had always made jokes like some kind of shield. In the process he had also kept other kids from getting close to him. At least until Jack had come along. He hadn't given Teddy much of a choice. They were going to be boys, Teddy just had to deal with it.

Now here they were, just the two of them, halftime in another one of their workouts. Sometimes Gus would join them. But he couldn't today: he had a doctor's appointment for his school physical. Jack and Teddy were planning to meet up with Gus and Cassie later and figure out how they wanted to spend one of their last days of summer vacation.

There was no real plan. They didn't need one, and that was one of the best parts of summer. It was practically a rule that you had nowhere you really needed to be until the first day of school. Or the first day of football practice.

Provided you made the team, of course.

This year Teddy couldn't separate the start of school and the start of football in his head. He'd been marking time from the end of baseball—and the parade down Main Street in Walton the mayor had organized for them when they'd gotten home from Williamsport—until football tryouts at Holzman.

Even with his great spring and summer in baseball, from the time he'd started working out with Jack, his dream was to be a football player.

In two days he would officially get his chance.

Football was why he had pushed himself to get into shape.

MIKE LUPICA

Football was Teddy's goal. Jack said you needed to set goals for yourself in sports. He was sure Teddy would be the starter for the Wildcats at tight end.

He told him that again now.

"How about I just make the team first?" Teddy said.

"You're going to make the team, you're going to start, you're going to be one of my primary receivers."

"Have you been out in the sun too long today?" Teddy said. "Are you starting to feel light-headed?"

Jack shrugged. "Make your little jokes," he said. "My parents just say I'm highly motivated."

"Or maybe just dehydrated?" Teddy said.

"You want to have that attitude?" Jack said, picking up the ball and jumping to his feet. "Go long, sucker."

Teddy tossed his Gatorade bottle aside. "I can do that," he said.

Running came easily to Teddy now, after all the laps he and Jack had been running on the track. Jack had even gotten Teddy doing his interval training: sprinting, then slowing down to a jog, then sprinting even harder than before.

When they'd finished the first time, Teddy had said to Jack, "I used to think intervals were just the time between snacks."

But in the late morning, the sun already high in the sky, Teddy ran as hard as he could, from rightfield toward left. He knew it was impossible to outrun Jack Callahan's right arm. So he just put his head down, trusting Jack would let him know when he should turn back for the ball.

"Now!" he heard Jack yell.

Teddy turned back and looked up at the same time, saw the ball in the air, another perfect spiral. He reached for it, secured it with his big hands—"mitts," Jack called them—and then pulled the ball tight to his chest.

Teddy kept running with the ball until he reached the fence in the left-field corner. In that moment he just wanted to keep going, run through the fence or try to jump over it. The feeling he had, he wanted that feeling to last, he wanted to imagine the green grass out here stretching out in front of him forever.

You always heard the announcers on television talking about receivers "running in space." That was what Teddy felt then. Like he was the one running in space.

Or just floating through it.

From the across the field Jack shouted, "Are you planning on coming back anytime soon?"

"If I come back," Teddy shouted back, "I know what you're going to say."

"What?"

"Go long again."

"Exactly!" Jack said.

When Teddy got back to him, he said to Jack, "You went a lot easier on me when you felt sorry for me."

"No way," Jack said. "You didn't need me to do that, because you were too busy feeling sorry for yourself."

"Excellent point."

The truth was, and they both knew it, they were both feeling pretty sorry for themselves when they first became friends, even though they didn't know that was what they were doing at the time. There was the day when Jack just got tired of the other guys picking on Teddy, how funny the other guys thought it was when Teddy ended up on the floor during a game of dodgeball. Jack went over and helped Teddy up, in more ways than one.

But around the same time, Teddy helped Jack get up too and stop blaming himself for his brother's accident. Teddy finally helped convince Jack that Brad Callahan, as reckless as he was, with dirt bikes and everything else, was an accident waiting to happen. Jack didn't need anybody to pick on him, because he was doing way too good a job beating himself up.

"I found out the hard way," Jack liked to say now. "It's not about getting knocked down, it's how you get back up."

He and Teddy had done that.

Together.

• • •

Jack threw Teddy another deep ball, telling him to angle toward the infield this time, like he was running a deep post pattern. On this one, Teddy had to slow down a little to catch the ball in stride.

"Arm getting a little tired there," he said.

"We'll see how tired I look the next time I knock you over with a short pass," Jack said.

That was the thing about Jack. As cool a kid as he was, he was cocky, too. He just managed to do a good job hiding it from people. But it was always there.

"I take it back!" Teddy said, laughing. "Please don't hurt me!"

Teddy knew the drill with Jack Callahan: you were never just throwing the ball around. There was a purpose to everything he did. To him, this was a real practice. So they ran some short slants, the ones Jack was sure would be in their playbook this season. Jack practiced taking a one-step drop after being snapped the ball by an imaginary center, straightening up, hitting Teddy in the gut with passes that sometimes knocked the wind out of him.

They alternated those with quick outs. Then Jack told Teddy to go deep again. When they decided to stop for good, they stretched out on their backs in the outfield grass, both out of breath.

They were silent for a while, feeling the sun on their faces, until Jack said, "How much taller are you than when you started seventh grade?"

"My mom says four inches. Maybe five."

"You, my friend, are going to be a matchup nightmare. You're built like a tight end, but you're as fast as a wide receiver."

"How about we find out if I can catch like this at the try-outs before you send me to the Hall of Fame in Canton?" Teddy said. "Did it ever occur to you that maybe I'm not ready for this? It's not like I *made* the baseball team. I just turned out to be an emergency catcher after Scott Sutter got hurt."

Jack propped his head up in his hand and looked at him. "Blah, blah, blah," he said. "When the old Teddy starts talking, I can't hear a word."

Teddy nodded. "Old habits."

"Forget about old habits, or the old Teddy. You can do this. We can do it together."

"We're a team now."

"Just like baseball," Jack said. "I pitch, you catch."

Jack said he'd wait while Teddy dropped the ball off at his house, and then they'd call Gus and Cassie and meet them at Cassie's. Teddy ran the short distance to his house, the ball under his arm again. He smiled as he ran, knowing he should feel tired, but not feeling tired at all.

He just felt happy.

At least he did until he got to his back porch, looked up, and saw his father standing there.

"Hey, champ," David Madden said.

TWO

The next afternoon Teddy and his three friends were at the pond near Cassie Bennett's house. They lay on the dock, all of them in their bathing suits, having just gone for another swim.

Cassie Bennett always asked the most questions, about everything. Today was no different.

"This is really happening?" she said. "Your dad's moving back here?"

"He *has* moved back."

"And you didn't know until yesterday?"

Teddy shook his head.

Cassie said, "And he didn't tell your mom, either?"

"He said he wanted it to be a surprise," Teddy said. He spread out his arms, put a fake smile on his face, and shouted "Surprise!" the way you did at a surprise party.

"Unbelievable," she said.

"Gee, you *think*?"

"And you're not happy about this?" Jack said.

"Do I sound happy?"

Jack let that one go.

They all sat there in silence for a moment, all of them on towels, staring up into sun and blue sky. Only it didn't feel like much of a blue-sky day to Teddy.

"And what did he say to you, mostly?" Gus said.

"He said he wanted to make this a new beginning for us," Teddy said. "I asked him when we'd ever had an old beginning."

His father had moved to Oregon to take a job in sales for Nike. Now he had gotten a better offer from ESPN, which had a new office about a half hour away. Teddy had driven by it one time, when Jack's parents had taken them to a water park down the road from what everybody called the new ESPN "campus."

But Teddy's dad wasn't going to live near his new office. He was going to live in Walton.

"How does your mom feel about this?" Cassie said. "She can't be happy."

"She wasn't happy or sad or angry or anything," Teddy said. "She just said that we're all going to have to make this work. And that she hoped I would give him a chance. I asked her when he'd ever given me a chance."

"Well, then that's what we're going to have to do!" Cassie said.

Somehow she had gotten off her back and was sitting cross-legged facing him.

"*We?*" Teddy said.

"Yup," she said. "We. Because we are all in this together. Right?"

Jack knew enough to say "Right." When Gus hesitated, Cassie smacked him on the shoulder. "*Right?*" she said to him.

"Right," Gus said. "And ouch."

"Tell me again, how many times have you seen him since he and your mom got divorced?" Cassie asked. "Ballpark number."

Teddy said, "I think six times in eight years."

Cassie shook her head. "I get how far away he lived. But that's like somebody pretending that airplanes haven't been invented."

"Just about every time it was because he had to be back on business."

"And he doesn't call?"

"At first he did. Until he started to figure out that he didn't have anything to say to me."

"What was yesterday like?"

"He didn't have much once he got past calling me 'champ.' Which I have now decided I like even less than Teddy Bear."

Gus sat up. Teddy knew that being from a close-knit family, Gus understood as much about growing up without a father around as he did about being an astronaut. It was probably why he had been so quiet today.

"Does he send you stuff on your birthday, or Christmas?" Gus said.

"He's the league leader in Amazon gift certificates. I've got a nice collection of them saved up."

"You've never used them?" Gus said.

"Nope," Teddy said. "I could never figure out whether they were gifts or bribes. And then I decided they weren't nearly big enough to be bribes. Now instead of a gift certificate, I'm getting *him*."

"Maybe he's changed," Jack said.

"He's changed *jobs*," Teddy said. "He's changed location. That's it."

Jack said, "You've gotten through everything else; you'll get through this. And like Cassie said, we'll help you."

"You know what this doesn't help me with?" Teddy said. "Making the Wildcats tomorrow."

"Shut up," Cassie said.

"Excuse me?" Teddy said.

"Shut . . . up," she said. "One has nothing to do with the other."

"Easy for you to say," he said.

"She's right," Jack said. He grinned. "As much as I hate saying that."

"You should be getting used to it by now," Cassie said.

"No," Jack said, "I mean it. This isn't going to get in your way, because nothing is going to get in your way."

"Then how come I feel like somehow my own dad has tackled me from behind?" Teddy said.

Cassie smiled. "Because he did?"

"No wonder you get good grades."

"Don't you feel better now?" she said.

"*No!*" Teddy said. Then he said, "Can we change the subject?"

"*No!*" they all yelled back at him.

The truth was, he didn't feel any better today than he had last night about his dad moving back to Walton, moving back into his life, no matter how much his friends were trying to get him to laugh his way past the whole thing. He was still angry, he was still confused, he still *hated* his dad blindsiding him and his mom the way he had. He told Jack and Cassie and Gus now that knowing his dad, it really was a surprise that he'd told them in person, and not tweeted out the news instead.

"Hundred and forty characters," Teddy said. "He could have summed up our whole relationship in that many. The dad from Twitter."

"I thought you wanted to stop talking about this," Cassie said.

"Now I do."

And they did. The only thing that made him feel better was being with them. It didn't matter to Teddy that Jack might look at Gus, or even Cassie, as his best friend. Or that Gus might feel closer to Jack. Teddy just felt close to all of them, never closer than he did right now. Over these last months, as he had become stronger and more confident—as much as that confidence had gotten rocked yesterday when he'd seen his father standing there, big smile on his face, on the porch—Teddy had figured something out:

You kept score in sports, not friendships.

On this day, more than ever, he was getting as much as he needed from his friends, and that was all that mattered. A few minutes later, they went for another swim. When they got out,

Jack and Gus started to talk about tomorrow's tryouts, and Teddy allowed himself to get carried along by their excitement about the next season starting for all of them.

Before long, a lot of the afternoon sun was gone, and so was the afternoon. It was time for all of them to head home for dinner. They dropped Cassie off at her corner. Gus had left his bike at her house, so the two of them walked down her street together.

Just Teddy and Jack now.

"We've still got an hour," Jack said.

Teddy knew exactly what he meant.

"You go get your sneakers," Teddy said. "I'll go get the ball."

He ran most of the way home, not sure whether he was running away from something or not.

THREE

Teddy and Jack played until Teddy's mom called to him from the backyard that it really was time for dinner, even though today Teddy would have been willing to catch passes from Jack until it got too dark.

"You're ready," Jack said as Teddy was leaving.

"For anything?"

"Yeah," Jack said. "For anything."

When he got into the house, the first thing he said to his mom was, "Is he here?"

"No," she said, "he is not."

"Just the two of us for dinner?" Teddy said, feeling relieved.

"You and me, kid." She told him to go get cleaned up, their food would be ready in fifteen minutes.

Once Teddy had decided to get into shape, his mom started cooking healthier meals, limiting red meat to once or twice a week, if that. Tonight was red snapper and green beans on the side and a salad. Teddy was happy to have it, even though there had been a time when he would have been happy eating cheeseburgers and fries every night.

They spent most of the early part of their dinner talking about a letter that all school parents had received that day, telling them that because of budget cuts in Walton, various programs were about to be cut in the town's public schools. The most serious in his mom's mind was that Mrs. Brandon's music department at Walton Middle School would be closed down at the end of this semester. There was even talk of canceling the big holiday show that Mrs. Brandon staged every year before winter break.

"But everybody loves Mrs. Brandon," Teddy said. "Even I like the holiday show."

"I went to school with her," his mom said. "We even had a girl group back in the day."

"No way."

"Way," she said. "We called ourselves the Baubles."

"You're making this up."

"I wish," she said, grinning. "There was a popular girl group back in the day called the Bangles."

"The secret life of Mom," he said.

She shook her head. "I have to think of something," she said. "For kids who love music, this would be like cutting a sports team."

"What can you do?" Teddy said.

"Something."

They ate in silence for a few minutes.

"By the way?" Teddy's mom said. "I still feel terrible about yesterday. I should have come out to the field and told you myself that he was here."

"What, and spoil his big moment?"

"It's who he is," she said. "It's who he's always been. Maybe that's why he's such a good salesman. He thinks presentation is everything."

"He actually thinks that was the way to announce he was coming back here?"

"He always loved drama, too."

"So now he's brought it all the way across the country," Teddy said. "Maybe we should have given him a standing O yesterday."

"You're going to have to get used to it. We both are."

"I like things the way they are, Mom," Teddy said. "I never felt cheated because I didn't live with both parents. I had you."

"You're sweet."

He grinned, feeling like himself for a minute. "Let's not get carried away."

"I never asked you last night," she said. "How did it go when it was just the two of you talking?"

"Once he got past telling me how excited he was to be back, he pretty much had nothing. Other than asking me to give him a second chance."

"You have to," she said.

"No, I don't," Teddy said. "I didn't get a vote when he left, I didn't get a vote when he decided to move back. This is one thing I get to decide. He doesn't get to play dad now because it will make him feel better."

"I'm more interested in what you're feeling," she said.

"I don't think you need to be a mind reader to figure that out."

There was a silence between them. Both of them were done eating. Neither made a move to clear their plates. It was as if they had reached some kind of standoff. Teddy just wasn't sure about what.

He said, "I can't believe he shows up right before tryouts."

"I'm not asking you to be thrilled, Teddy. I'm not asking you to even like it right now. But what I'm asking you to do is try to make this work for me."

Teddy slapped his hand on the table. "I'm supposed to be nice to him for *you*?" he said. "When was *he* ever nice to you?"

There was another silence. Usually he loved this time with his mom. He would tell her about his day. She'd tell him about hers. They were both good talkers. He felt like he'd inherited that from her, the way he'd inherited whatever else that was good in him.

Alexis Madden would ask Teddy sometimes—though not so much lately—if he could remember things they'd done as a family when David Madden was still around. Teddy would answer truthfully: No. He really couldn't. He didn't know if it was because he was too little, or because he was trying to block those memories out.

"Teddy," she said, "I know it's hard, but . . ."

She reached across the table and covered Teddy's hand with her own.

"Promise me you'll try to be open-minded," she said. "And

openhearted. I know it's asking a lot. But this isn't him asking. It's me."

He stared at her, afraid she might start to cry. What he did remember, from the time his dad left, as young as he'd been? He remembered his mom crying a lot.

"I'll try," he said. "I can't promise that this deal is going to work out the way he might want it to. But I'll try."

She told him she'd clean up; he should go upstairs and rest. He had a big day tomorrow.

"I don't know how many more big days I can stand this week," Teddy said.

He thought about calling Jack when he got upstairs, but after the dock, and after dinner with his mom, he was talked out for today. As he lay on his bed, staring at the ceiling, not even paying attention to the songs he was listening to on his speakers, he kept coming back to this one thought:

Having a dad in his life *was* something that should have made him happy.

He had real friends now, he had teammates, he had football, he'd been good enough in sports, in a pretty short time, to have been the starting catcher on a team that played in the Little League World Series. Now he had a shot at making the

Wildcats, and if Jack Callahan was right—and he was usually right about sports—he had a chance to be the team's starting tight end. Having a dad should have been like icing on top of a big old cake.

Not everybody he knew at Walton Middle School had a full-time dad in their lives. A couple of other kids who'd be starting eighth grade with him had divorced parents. But most kids he knew, and most of the guys he played sports with, usually had a dad around to cheer them on.

He'd never needed a dad before. He didn't need one tomorrow at Holzman Field.

He just wanted to make the team.

FOUR

Teddy was more grateful than ever that Jack had worked him out as hard as he had since the end of baseball.

Because the tryouts were beyond intense.

"I think this is what guys in the Marines call basic training," Gus said to Teddy and Jack about an hour into it. "And we're not even in pads today!"

"No," Teddy said, "I think basic training would feel like a vacation compared to this."

"Do I hear complaining?" Jack said.

"Just making an observation," Teddy said. "A very, very tired observation, and we've only been here an hour."

"You just *think* you're tired," Jack said. "Actually you're about to catch your second wind."

"If I am trying to catch it," Teddy said, "I hope it's not moving too quickly."

They had just run sprints and intervals and laps so far, being watched and evaluated by parents from Walton Town Football who didn't have a son trying out for the team. And they were being watched by the man who'd coach the Wildcats, Dick Gilbert.

Andre Williams's dad, Malik, an outside linebacker who'd gone from Walton High to Wake Forest to the pros for a few seasons, was observing from the stands. He wasn't allowed to officially evaluate because Andre was trying out, even though Mr. Williams was going to be Coach Gilbert's defensive coordinator. But everybody was pretty sure that Andre, who'd been a pitcher and outfielder on the Rays, was going to be a starter at outside linebacker—and a star at the position—the same as his dad.

After all the running, they moved to agility drills. One was called the step over. Blocking bags were set up a few feet apart, and the players had to run through the bags, high-stepping over them the way they would a downed blocker during a game. Coach Gilbert told them that when he'd been a wide receiver at Walton High, getting over players who'd been blocked to the ground was called "getting through the trash."

"Of course, once the season starts," he said, "the trash on the ground will be somebody else's, not ours."

When they came back from a brief water break, they lined up and zigzagged their way through orange cones that were set up on the field, the parents and Coach Gilbert wanting to see how they could handle quick cuts.

Finally they were separated out by size and the position they wanted to play. Teddy was surprised at how many of the bigger kids said they wanted to play in the line, either offensive or defensive.

But he quickly figured out what was happening: kids *really* wanted to make this team, and not end up in Pop Warner. And even if they secretly wanted to run with the ball or catch it or throw it, they were going for the positions they thought gave them their best chance at making the Walton Wildcats. Coach Gilbert reminded them all, more than once, that the ultimate decision about where guys were going to play would be his.

Gus went over with the wide receivers. Jack had predicted that Gus would probably end up being the kind of slot receiver Victor Cruz had been for the Giants before he hurt his knee.

There were three other kids trying out for tight end with Teddy. One was Mike O'Keeffe, a good guy they'd played against in baseball.

"Good luck," he said to Teddy when it was time for the receiving drills, and Teddy knew Mike meant it.

"Jack says it's not about luck," Teddy said.

"Yeah," Mike said. "But he's Jack."

Every boy trying out today had been given a blue mesh practice jersey with big white numbers on the front and back, to make things easier for the evaluators. By chance Teddy had been given number 81. Megatron's number. Calvin Johnson of the Lions. Teddy didn't care. He was a Giants fan, which meant he was an Odell Beckham Jr. guy.

There were two other kids trying out for quarterback along with Jack. Danny Hayes was an eighth grader and had a good arm, but he was a better runner than he was a passer. And there was a seventh grader who'd just moved to Walton during the summer, a kid named Bruce Kalb. Bruce was almost as big as Teddy and seemed to have a pretty big arm himself. But if he did make the team, the best he could hope for was to be Jack's backup. Nobody was beating out Jack.

When Coach Gilbert walked them down to the other end of the field for the passing and receiving drills, Jack and Gus walked with Teddy.

Jack said, "Just pretend it's the two of us in the outfield."

"That's going to be hard when you're not the one throwing to me," Teddy said.

There were going to be three rounds; each quarterback would make the throws in one of them.

"You can still pretend it's me," Jack said.

"This is going to be cake," Gus said, grinning as he added, "Not that you eat much cake anymore."

It wasn't cake.

Coach lined up receivers on both sides of the field. Each receiver would get four balls thrown to him with nobody covering: first a slant, then a curl, a deep post pattern, a straight fly down the sideline.

On the fifth throw, one of the other kids in the line would come out to cover, and you were supposed to do whatever you thought you had to do to get open.

Teddy was hoping for Jack the first time through but got Bruce Kalb instead. Teddy caught the slant pass just fine, Bruce leading him beautifully. But then he missed the next three, the ball either going off his hands or through them all three times. It felt like his hands were on backward.

When Mike O'Keeffe came out to cover him, Teddy gave him a good head fake to the outside and got inside position. He cut to the middle of the field, about twenty yards from Bruce. But the ball was slightly underthrown. Mike read it better—and sooner—than Teddy did.

Mike stepped in and intercepted the ball cleanly.

"Gotta fight for that ball," Coach Gilbert said. "Gotta want it, eighty-one."

Then he turned away, blew his whistle, and said, "Next."

Teddy put his head down, ran to the back of the line on the opposite side of the field, felt himself clenching and unclenching his fists, worried that he might have blown his shot at making the team already.

He didn't realize Gus was behind him until he heard Gus say, "Remember what Aaron Rodgers said to Packers fans that time after he played, like, his worst game? R-E-L-A-X."

"I *can't*," Teddy said. "You know how Coach just said you gotta want it? I want it too much."

"Just let it happen," Gus said.

"I'm gonna happen myself right into Pop Warner," Teddy said. "That's what's gonna happen."

He didn't get Jack in the next round either, getting Danny Hayes instead. Teddy didn't do much better this time. The slant bounced off his shoulder pad, Danny threw high on the curl. When he tried to run his fly pattern, Teddy stumbled as he reached for the ball and ended up doing a solid, gold-plated face-plant.

He did get up and manage to make a catch in coverage. Danny threw high again as Teddy came back a little for the ball, but Teddy was able to go up as high as he could and get his hands on the ball and keep them there.

But he knew all Coach and the other parents were going to remember was him falling down.

I waited all summer for this, he thought.

All year, really.

And now I can't even get out of my own way.

Before the last round, Coach gave them another water break. Jack came over and pulled Teddy away from where the other kids were getting their drinks.

"I'm thirsty," Teddy said.

"Not now, you're not," Jack said.

He walked him even farther away, so nobody could hear them.

"I know what you're thinking," Jack said.

"No, you don't."

"Yes, I do," Jack said. "But this thing isn't over yet. You can still pull this out."

"Every other kid on this field is playing better than me," Teddy said.

"Not true," Jack said. "That last catch you made, hardly anybody out here could go up and get it like that. You're still bigger than the other guys at your position, you're still fast. And you've still got great hands."

"Hands of stone."

Jack ignored him. "And now you've got me coming out of the bull pen to throw to you, which means the way I've been throwing to you at school, and the way I'll be throwing to you all season."

"You headed down to Pop Warner too?" Teddy said.

Then Gus was with them. It was the same as always. All for one.

"Well," Gus said, "he may have a lousy attitude, but he hasn't lost his sense of humor."

"Well, and my mind," Teddy said.

This time around he would be the last to go. So he watched Gus catch all five balls Jack threw to him, and Mike O'Keeffe do the same.

Mike went right before Teddy. As he was running back with the football, Jack jogged over, leaned close to Teddy, and said, "On your last one, when the guy is covering you, I want you to do something for me."

"What?"

Jack grinned. "Go long," he said.

"You want *that* to be the last thing Coach is going to see today?"

"Yup," Jack said. "Stop. And go long."

Teddy told himself to focus all his attention, and all his energy, on Jack; told himself to remember all their sessions behind Walton Middle, all the hours they'd spent together. He told himself to forget Coach and the evaluators and all the other kids watching.

Just me and Jack, he told himself.

He pitches, I catch.

Simple.

He ran his slant. Jack didn't baby him, drilling a pass into Teddy's stomach. Then Teddy ran his next three patterns—curl, post, fly—and caught them all. He was trying to think along with Jack now. Maybe Jack wanted him to go long again because Mike O'Keeffe, guarding him again, wouldn't be expecting two straight deep throws.

"Last play of the day," Coach Gilbert called out. "Let's make 'er a good one."

It wasn't just the last play of the day, it was Teddy's last chance to impress him, to show him how much game he really had.

His last chance to show Coach he belonged.

Teddy knew Mike would try as hard as he could to pick

another ball off or knock one down. Maybe in his mind, a stop here might mean he made the team and Teddy didn't. Maybe it would be all that was separating them when the evaluators and Coach added everything up.

Teddy would have looked at things exactly the same way if he was the one on defense.

"*Go!*" Coach yelled.

Teddy took off down the right sideline, head down, running hard. When he suddenly put the brakes on, Mike jammed up on him, as if sure Jack was going to deliver the ball right there.

Teddy had him.

He took a big first step and was in high gear again, like a car going from zero to sixty. In that moment he had three full steps on Mike. It was like he was running free in the outfield at Walton Middle, right behind his own house.

When he turned around, Teddy saw that Jack had put some air under the ball, more than the throw before. He wanted to give Teddy every chance to run under it.

Teddy could see it all now: Ball and sky and Mike O'Keeffe, his own head down, trying to get back into the play, to give himself a chance to *make* a play.

But Teddy wasn't watching Mike, he was watching the flight of the ball.

One that he was sure now that Jack had overthrown.

It just looked too high and too deep and too far out of his reach.

Teddy knew he had to be close to the end zone. He just didn't know how close. He turned almost all the way around, knowing that this wasn't a ball he could run through. He had to jump for it.

He jumped, reaching up as high as he could, feeling as if he were starting to fall backward as he did, trying to make his right arm longer than it really was.

At the last possible moment he put up his big right hand, one of those mitts, like he was trying to touch the sky.

He didn't catch the ball cleanly, the way his man Beckham had that time against the Cowboys, what everybody had called the greatest catch of all time.

But as Teddy felt the ball touch his hand and felt himself falling back to earth at the same time, he controlled the ball just enough to tip it forward, tip it into his body, so he could somehow get his left hand on it too.

As he landed on his back—hard—he knew both hands were on the ball Jack had just thrown him.

He was aware, even flat on his back, that it had gotten kind of loud at Holzman Field.

He was still on his back, the ball still pressed to his chest, when he looked up and saw Jack Callahan staring down at him.

Teddy thought he shouldn't have been able to get down the field that fast.

But he was Jack.

"That ought to work," he said to Teddy.

Then he was pulling Teddy up.

Again.

FIVE

This was the way Coach Gilbert left it with them before they left tryouts:

He would meet that night with the evaluators, and then he would post the names of the kids who had made the Wildcats on the Walton Town Football website at eleven o'clock the next morning. The rest of the kids would find their names on the town's Pop Warner site. Then he asked that the kids who made the Wildcats show up at Holzman Field at one o'clock, where they'd be given game jerseys, helmets, pads, and playbooks.

Then they had to go to Bob's Sports and try on their football pants there.

Teddy and Jack and Gus decided they wanted to be together—all for one—when they found out, even though Teddy knew there was no real drama for his friends. They were making the team; they'd both played like total stars.

Cassie was with them too. She never wanted to be left out of anything.

She said, "I'm just here for the drama."

The next day, they met up at Jack's house at nine thirty. Mrs. Callahan made them all pancakes. It was ten when Jack grabbed his laptop and they went down to the basement to wait through what Teddy knew was going to be the longest hour of his life.

At least he wasn't thinking about his dad today. Just about football. Because right now football mattered more to him.

"Stop worrying," Cassie said. "You're all going to make it."

"We *are* all going to make it," Gus said.

"I know Cassie doesn't know what she's talking about," Teddy said.

"*Hey,*" she said.

"But you were there," Teddy said to Gus. "You saw how I played before I made one lucky catch."

Cassie said, "I heard it was a little more than luck. Jack and Gus said you morphed into that guy from the Giants who stole David Beckham's name."

"I don't think he stole it, exactly," Jack said.

"He's going to make it, right?" Gus said to Jack. "I'm right, right?"

Jack grinned. "Right," he said.

"You're being serious, right?" Gus said.

"I am being serious," Jack said. "Coach isn't going to cut a guy who made that catch."

"I still can't believe I caught it," Teddy said.

"And do you know why you did?"

"No. But I know I'm about to find out."

"Because you had to," Jack said. "Sometimes in sports you're better than you think you are, because you have to be."

Teddy didn't want to check his phone again to see what time it was, but it was as if Gus were reading his mind.

"Five till," he said.

Jack turned on the television. They tried to watch *SportsCenter*. Teddy knew they were both acting nervous just to make him *less* nervous. It wasn't working. But they had to try. There were about a million ways, he was discovering, to be a good friend.

Or a great one.

The list wasn't finally posted until ten minutes after eleven o'clock.

"Wait," Jack said.

"*Wait?*" Teddy said. "Because we're all having so much fun here?"

"No," Jack said, shaking his head. "I can't access the list."

"Let me try," Cassie said. "You're probably doing something wrong."

"Yeah," Jack said, his fingers moving across the keys, "only *you* have a handle on this whole Internet thing."

"Well," she said, "if you don't want help . . ."

"I don't."

"Would it be helpful," Teddy said, "if I reminded you again that I am dying here?"

"I'm doing my best," Jack said.

It took him nearly five more minutes, which made all the other waiting time since Teddy had awakened this morning feel as if it had gone by in a blink.

Finally Jack exhaled, then said in a quiet voice, "Here it is."

Gus walked over the arm of his chair and jumped on the couch next to him. Cassie got on the other side.

Teddy didn't move.

Nobody said anything until Jack Callahan looked up, smiling at Teddy. Pointing at the screen.

"Callahan, Jack," he said. "Madden, Teddy. Morales, Gus."

It got even louder in the basement than it had the day before at Holzman when Teddy had come down with the ball.

Make the catch, make the team.

It was a good, loud, happy scene at Holzman Field a couple of hours later, one table set up with uniform jerseys on them, another one with helmets and pads.

Teddy hadn't even asked about team colors, mostly because he didn't think he'd get this far. But he couldn't believe what he saw:

Giants colors.

Blue helmets, with a small, white Walton *w* on the side, like the lowercase *ny* on Giants helmets. Old-school all the way. And the jerseys were dark blue, like the Giants' road jerseys.

The colors for his favorite team were now his colors, on his team.

Some of the kids didn't care what number they got, some kids did. The guys in the line, offense and defense, seemed willing to take anything in the 60s or 70s. Jack requested number 12 and got it, because he loved Aaron Rodgers and loved Tom Brady, too. Teddy just waited. He felt as if he had to have been one of the last guys picked, like the last kid picked in a playground game.

So he was just going to wait his turn, take whatever was left when he got up to the table.

But when he did get up there, Coach Gilbert was smiling at him. He had a jersey in his hands, but Teddy couldn't see the number.

"Congratulations," Coach said.

"Thanks, Coach."

"I think I mentioned yesterday that I was a receiver in high school," he said. "As a matter of fact, I used to catch passes from your dad."

"My mom told me that," Teddy said, "when I told her you were coaching the Wildcats."

"Well, in my *life*, I never made a catch like you made yesterday, son," he said. He paused and said, "I asked some of the other parents, and they told me you've never played organized football before. Is that true?"

"No, sir," Teddy said. "I never did." He grinned at Coach, the old Teddy coming out of him, and added, "Mostly because nobody would have me."

"Well, I will," Coach Gilbert said.

"Thank you," Teddy said. "I wish the season was starting today."

"Got a number preference?" Coach said.

Teddy ducked his head, looked up, and said, "Actually, I do."

MIKE LUPICA

"One of your buddies might have mentioned you were a Giants fan."

"Big-time," Teddy said.

"Do I even have to guess who your favorite player is?"

"Number thirteen," Teddy said.

"Had a feeling," Coach said, and then handed him the jersey in his hands.

13.

Teddy looked at the jersey and the number and then back at Coach. "Thank you *so* much!" he said.

"It's all yours," Coach said. "Pretty much been yours since you made that catch yesterday."

Teddy thanked him again and walked away with the jersey, feeling as if Coach Gilbert had just handed him some kind of trophy.

He got his helmet next, got fitted for his pads, grabbed a playbook off the stack. It was a long walk home from Holzman if you were carrying this much stuff. Jack said his dad could drive Teddy. Teddy said he wanted to walk, and that he'd call Jack later.

He didn't remember much of the walk, just that it felt like he was floating, all the way past school, cutting across the outfield, across his backyard, through the back door, placing his uniform carefully on the kitchen table.

This time his dad was waiting for him in the living room.

SIX

His mom was sitting on the sofa, her hands in her lap. She was smiling, but Teddy got the idea that her smile was something she'd put on, like her makeup.

Just from what he'd observed the other day, she was a different person when his dad was around.

His *dad*.

It was one more thing he didn't have a choice about, thinking of him that way, whether he wanted to or not. But how else was he going to think of him? Mr. Madden?

Dave?

Teddy went over and sat down next to his mom.

"Hey, champ," David Madden said. "How did it go today?"

Teddy wanted to tell his mom the good news, but he didn't want to do it with his father in the room, the guy who thought it was cool calling him "champ." He had called Teddy that the other day on the porch. It was what he called Teddy on the phone.

Teddy hated it more than ever. What had just happened at Holzman, he wasn't a part of it. It wasn't his. *It's mine,* Teddy thought. *Mine and Mom's.*

"I was in the neighborhood," his dad said.

Teddy waited.

"I just wanted to stop by because I didn't feel as if we really got much of a chance to talk the other day," his dad said.

"Not much to talk *about,*" Teddy said.

"Well, truth be told, there's a lot to talk about," David Madden said. "Not that we have to do it all right away."

"I'm definitely down with that," Teddy said.

"I understand this is a lot for you to process."

"You understand," Teddy said, nodding. "You mean, like you understand me?"

"Teddy," his mom said in a low, strained voice.

"No, Alexis," his dad said. "The boy and I need to talk this out."

From champ to boy. *Wow,* Teddy thought, *I'm starting to lose ground here.*

"Is that what we're doing?" Teddy said. "Really? Talking things out? Like a real father-son talk?"

David Madden said, "Listen, Teddy, I know our relationship is obviously going to change."

Now Teddy couldn't help himself, whether he was going to upset his mom or not. "*What* relationship?"

"Teddy," she said again, even quieter than before.

"You're right," his dad said. "A hundred percent. I should have said that we're going to start a relationship, at least if that's all right with you. You might not want that, at least not right away. But I do. I know I can't undo the past, and that's on me. But I'm here now."

Teddy took a closer look at him than he had when he'd first come to the house. His father had more gray hair than the last time he'd seen him. He looked older, somehow.

"You're not here because of me," Teddy said. "You're here because you got a better job."

David Madden put his hands up, almost in surrender.

"Listen," he said. "I know this is going to be uncomfortable, for all of us, at least at the beginning. All I'm asking is for you, again, to give me a chance to make things right."

"You never gave me a chance," Teddy said. "Why should I give you one?"

"Because I'm your dad and I'm asking you," David Madden said. "You may not think I've earned the right. I probably *haven't* earned the right. All I'm asking you to do is have an open mind, and judge me on what I do from now on."

"A daddy do-over?" Teddy said. He had a fake smile of his own going now.

"I know you're being sarcastic, but yeah, something like that," his dad said. "Like I said, I'm just looking for a fresh start here."

That was it. Teddy stood up. "When was our first start?" he said.

He walked across the room, got to the doorway, turned, and said, "Good talk, though."

Then he couldn't help himself.

"Oh, I almost forgot," he added. "I made the team."

SEVEN

The Wildcats' first game was Saturday, at home, against the Hollis Hills Bears.

Hollis Hills was about an hour away. At least half the teams in their league were that far away, so the guys on the team knew they were going to do some traveling this season for All-American Football. They didn't care. The idea of longer road trips just made the whole thing seem even more glamorous, like they really were playing in the big leagues.

There were nine teams in the league, which meant eight games in the regular season. If they won their league, they qualified for the district final. Beyond that, details about the postseason were sketchy. Because this was a start-up program, even Coach Gilbert wasn't sure what would happen if they won the district.

"They're figuring it out as they go along," he'd said the night before at practice. "But here's the way I figure it, and so should you: if we win enough games, good things will happen."

It was *all* good as far as Teddy Madden, number 13, was concerned. He was learning more about being a tight end with every practice, about how to run the cleanest patterns, how to throw the best blocks, even how to be a good decoy when the ball was going to Gus or Mike O'Keeffe or even one of the guys coming out of the back field.

And he felt as if he and Jack were reading each other's minds even better than when Teddy was Jack's first option as a receiver. Teddy couldn't speak for everybody else on the team. But one thing he knew for certain was that he and the quarterback were ready for Hollis Hills.

The last practice before the game was on Thursday night, full pads, offense against the defense, everybody into it, everybody on the field treating it like a real game, nobody wanting to give an inch.

About an hour into it, Gus said to Teddy, "Is this fun or what?"

"You think pads and helmets are enough tonight," Teddy said, "or should we have asked for body armor?"

But he knew he was loving it the way everybody else on the team was. The way they were all getting after it just made him want to play Hollis Hills *right now.*

Then he looked over and saw his dad standing on the sidelines next to Coach Gilbert.

They had already run their red-zone offense, and their two-minute drill. Coach told the offense to start at its own twenty yard line and run the first ten plays he planned to run on this same field against the Bears on Saturday morning.

While they waited for Coach Williams to give the defense some last-minute instructions, Teddy just kept staring at his dad and Coach Gilbert.

"What's he doing here?" Teddy said.

"What is who doing here?" Gus said, following Teddy's eyes to the sideline.

"My dad."

Gus said, "No kidding, that's him over there with Coach?"

"The man, the legend," Teddy said.

He was wearing shorts and a T-shirt and sneakers, and an

ancient-looking cap with the Walton lowercase *w* on the front. He poked Coach Gilbert now and said something, and the two of them laughed.

"Couple of boys," Teddy said, "just chopping it up."

"But they *are* boys, aren't they?" Jack said. "They did play on the same high school team, right?"

"That was a long time ago," Teddy said.

"Well, it looks like all he's doing is watching practice," Gus said.

"Yeah," Teddy said. *"Mine."*

"Listen," Jack said. "Don't worry about what's going on over there. Just what's going on out here."

"Easy for you to say."

"Who said anything about easy?" Jack said, leaning forward and bumping helmets with Teddy. "This is a contact sport, remember?"

"Focus, dog," Gus said.

Teddy looked at him. "Woof, woof."

David Madden wasn't the only dad at practice. A bunch of dads would show up from work when they started at six o'clock, as they had tonight. Sometimes they'd stay the whole two hours. Teddy knew these were the real football dads, a lot of them former players themselves, some who'd played at Walton High the way Coach Gilbert and Coach Williams had.

Even Cassie had shown up on her bike to watch the last hour of practice tonight, something she did from time to time. But then she was as much of a football fan as any girl Teddy had ever met.

She didn't just love the game. She knew the game.

"Guys think everything is a guy thing," she had told them one night when they were all together after practice. "They must have missed the memo about the NFL trying to attract more women to their audience."

Jack told the players that the first three plays were going to be running plays. And that if they made a first down, they were going to run three more running plays. Coach had told them that they were going to start the game against Hollis Hills as if the forward pass hadn't been invented. That way when Coach finally did turn Jack loose, the Bears wouldn't know what hit them.

So Teddy concentrated on blocking for Jake Mozdean and Brian McAuley, their two best backs, pretending he was one of the big boys in the offensive line. He loved it when he'd put a linebacker on the ground and Jake or Brian would get five extra yards. One of the things he'd already realized about playing tight end was that size and speed and strength could make you just as good a blocker as a receiver.

"That's what I'm talking about!" Coach Gilbert yelled after Jake had ripped off another ten-yard run. "When you're pushing them back like this, they're *all* skill positions!"

After eight straight running plays, the offense was finally facing its first third down, from the defense's thirty-eight yard line. Once they'd made a couple of first downs, Coach had been alternating Jake and Brian, sending them in with the plays.

When Jake got to the huddle now, he said to Jack, "Coach wants belly-and-go."

Teddy felt the excitement right away. It was his favorite play. Jack, who was great with the ball, was going to fake a hand-off to Jake, knowing the defense was expecting a run on short yardage. He didn't just want the guys in the defensive line, and the linebackers, to bite on the fake. He wanted to freeze the defensive backs just enough as Gus came across the field and set a legal pick on Gregg Leonard, the safety who was supposed to pick up Teddy.

If it worked, Teddy was supposed to break to the outside and then down the sideline.

That was where the "go" part of the play came in.

When they broke the huddle, Jack grabbed Teddy's arm, pulled him close, and quickly said, "Before you turn into a receiver, *look* like a blocker."

Teddy nodded.

As he took his position, he couldn't help himself: he looked over to where his dad was still standing next to Coach, and wondered if Coach had told him what play was coming.

Teddy made sure not to get himself so worked up that he jumped the snap count. Once the ball was snapped, he got low, as if he were targeting Max Conte at middle linebacker. But he kept his eyes on Gus, waiting for him to come across the field. And as soon as Gus got close enough to Gregg—Gus had to act like a receiver himself, or it was a penalty—Teddy immediately kicked it up a notch and broke to the outside, going behind Gregg Leonard right away.

He was running in space again, waiting for a throw from Jack Callahan.

Exactly where he wanted to be.

Before he even looked back for the ball, knowing how open he was, he told himself to focus only on the catch, not what he was going to do after it.

When he did turn around, he realized he had waited too long, because the ball was nearly on him. If he had waited even one more stride, the ball might have hit him right in the face mask.

He got his big hands up in time, though, and pulled the ball out of the sky. It was here that he almost *did* get ahead of himself, looking up the field at all the green in front of him before he had secured the ball.

He started to bobble it, feeling for one terrible moment as if he might drop it, even though there wasn't a defender within ten yards of him.

But he didn't drop it.

He felt as if he were juggling it forever before pressing it to the front of his jersey with both hands and running the rest of the way into the end zone.

When he turned back to look at the field, he thought about spiking the ball. He didn't. He'd told himself once he'd made the team that he was never going to be one of those hey-look-at-me guys.

Even though that was exactly what he wanted to yell back to the man still standing next to Coach Gilbert.

Hey, Dad.

Look at me.

When Teddy got to the sideline, Jack and Gus with him, his dad acted as if it were the most normal thing in the world for him to be here like this, watching his son play. Watching his son make the kind of play he'd just made on belly-and-go.

"You told me he was good," David Madden said to Coach Gilbert. "You didn't tell me he was in training to be Gronkowski."

Rob Gronkowski was the Patriots' tight end. Teddy was sure that his dad had no idea he was a Giants fan. It was one more thing he'd never asked about, one more thing to add to the long list.

"And this guy here," Teddy's dad said, pointing at Jack, "I think he might already have a better arm than I did when I was throwing it to his coach in the old days. And I *know* he's already a better ball handler."

"I doubt that, Mr. Madden," Jack said. "But thank you."

Teddy looked at his dad. He seemed completely comfortable, as if being on the field like this, hanging with the boys, had put him in some kind of comfort zone, even with Teddy.

"You guys got a few extra minutes?" Coach said.

Teddy looked at Jack and Gus. They nodded.

"Sure," Teddy said to Coach Gilbert.

"Watching that fake," Coach said, "Teddy's dad had an idea about a move he thought might work for Jack in a good spot, especially down near the goal line. You guys mind working with him?"

Now Teddy hesitated. He didn't want to do it. He didn't want his dad thinking that he could just show up here and immediately become part of the coaching staff, part of the team. But at the same time, he knew he couldn't say no, because that would just make him look bad in front of Coach.

So instead of looking at Coach, he forced a grin and looked at his dad and said, "Have I ever denied you anything?"

"I just thought it would be worth taking a look at before we call it a night," Coach said. He nudged David Madden with an elbow as he added, "This guy has forgotten more about offense than most other guys will ever know."

They all walked back to the end of the field where Teddy had caught the pass, Coach included.

"It's not rocket science," David Madden said. "It's just an old-fashioned naked bootleg. It doesn't work if the quarterback can't sell the fake and then hide the ball. But seeing Jack out there, he can do both."

He set the ball down on the five yard line. He told Gus to set up like a running back and told Teddy to line up on what would have been the right side of the line.

"It's almost like being a magician," Teddy's dad said, "using a little sleight of hand. But it's a lot like the play you guys just ran. Because they expected you to run the ball, that's what they thought they saw when Jack put the ball in that boy's stomach. But with the bootleg, you not only put it in there and take it back, but then you hide it on your hip, as you almost start jogging away from the play, like Coach has Jack do on most basic running plays."

Then he said, "Like this."

He took the snap from Coach Gilbert, Gus came forward, Teddy's dad put the ball right about Gus's belt buckle with his right hand. Gus leaned forward like Coach had taught them, covering the imaginary ball up with both arms as Teddy's dad put the ball behind his right hip, the arm looking as if it were just hanging there naturally, and jogged toward the sideline.

Teddy watched him and thought, *It's like he's still a player.*

His dad didn't pull the ball up until he was running toward the pylon at the corner of the goal line.

"If a corner or safety or linebacker sees it coming, or figures out what's happening," he said, "I run along the line of scrimmage as long as I can before I look to throw. Teddy? You hold your block as long as *you* can, before you start running toward the corner of the end zone. But most of the time, if the QB runs it right, he could walk into the end zone."

He told Jack to try it. The first time he did, as big as Jack's hands were for a twelve-year-old, he dropped the ball when he tried to hold it.

David Madden jogged over to him.

"Grip it like you're going to throw, fingers on the seams," he said. "There's no glue on the ball, it won't just stick to your leg if you press it there."

The second time, Teddy watching over his shoulder as he imagined himself slow-jamming his way into the end zone, he couldn't tell that Jack had the ball even though Teddy knew he had it.

　　　　　　　　　　　　　　　　　MIKE LUPICA

The third time they ran it, Teddy's dad—Coach Dad, all of a sudden—ran at Jack from where he'd been standing in the end zone and told him to stop and throw to Teddy, which he did, a soft, accurate spiral.

"Love it," Coach Gilbert said. "It goes into everybody's playbook tomorrow."

"Peyton Manning shocked the world running that last season," Cassie called out from the sideline. "Shocked the world."

She always stayed out of the way when real practice was going on. But she must have figured it was all right to get closer to the action with just her boys on the field.

Teddy's dad turned around. "Smart girl," he said.

"Just ask her," Teddy said.

"Is she a friend?"

"Her name is Cassie Bennett," Gus said. "Coolest girl in the eighth grade."

"She thinks on the planet," Teddy said.

David Madden gave her a wave and called back to Cassie, "I better tell ESPN to start keeping an eye on you now."

Cassie said, "I know these guys think they invented sports. But I watch more ESPN than they do."

"Hey," David Madden said, "maybe one of these days I can give you all a tour of the campus at ESPN."

"Like a college campus?" Cassie said.

"Just with satellite dishes," Teddy's dad said.

"I'm in if they are," Cassie said.

"Who knows," David Madden said, "maybe I'm talking to the next Hannah Storm."

If Teddy didn't know better, he would have sworn that not only was Cassie smiling, she might actually have been blushing.

"Hey, let's run it one more time," David Madden said. "There's one more wrinkle you can throw in, if they've shadowed both Jack and Teddy. Gus, or whoever the running back is, can run straight through the line if nobody tackles him, thinking he doesn't really have the ball. Trust me, if he gets into the secondary and everything else has broken down, he'll be standing all by himself under the goalposts." He turned to Coach. "Remember how we beat St. Luke's that time with the same play?"

"Do I ever," Coach said. "Chuck Cotter was scared that he might drop the ball, that's how open he was. He acted like you'd tossed him a baby."

Teddy's dad said, "Walton fourteen, St. Luke's thirteen."

They high-fived each other, as if the play had just happened. Then Teddy's dad grabbed the ball and told Coach Gilbert to go deep, the way Jack was always telling Teddy to do the same thing.

The pass he threw Coach looked great in the air, but then

MIKE LUPICA

Coach had to come back, because the ball just seemed to drop all of a sudden. Teddy looked over and saw his dad wince and grab his shoulder.

But when his dad saw Teddy staring at him, he grinned and said, "Timing's a little off after all these years."

"Yeah," Teddy said before looking away. "Timing's everything, right?"

When Coach got back to them, he nodded at Teddy's dad and said, "Guy needs work."

"Tell me about it," Teddy said.

His dad and Coach walked off, arms around each other's shoulders. Teddy and Jack and Gus watched them go. Cassie had come out to join them.

"That was kind of fun," Jack said.

"Was it?" Teddy said.

"C'mon," Gus said, "you can see he's still got the moves."

"Yeah," Teddy said, "that's my dad. The guy with all the moves."

"He seemed nice," Cassie said.

"Why, because he thinks you're going to be a television star someday?" Teddy said.

Then he turned to look at all of them at once.

"You liked him, right?"

They hesitated, as if they weren't sure what the right answer was. Then they all nodded.

"You can't like him," Teddy said.

He took off his helmet and walked away, trying to calm down. He knew his friends hadn't done anything wrong. He knew he wasn't really mad at them. He was mad at his dad, out here trying as hard with them as he was with him, another time when he looked and acted like a salesman trying to make a sale. Of himself.

It had taken him only one practice, and it was as if his dad were already in midseason form.

EIGHT

After their last class on Friday, all of them having made it through the first-week grind of starting school, Cassie came over to Teddy when they were at their lockers and said, "Walk home from school with me."

She didn't even try to make it sound like a request, just like a play she had called.

"You are aware," Teddy said, "that I live right here and you live in the other direction, right?"

"Don't look at it as you going out of your way," she said. "Look at it as an opportunity to spend quality time with me alone."

Teddy slapped his forehead. "Why didn't I see that right away?"

"You're a guy?" she said.

"I knew it must be something like that," Teddy said. "Again."

Jack and Gus were spending some time after school at the assisted-living facility, as part of the community service hours for eighth graders. You had to have a certain amount of community service hours when you got to eighth grade, and Jack and Gus were getting the jump on that today. Then they were all meeting later for pizza and a movie.

Teddy would never admit it to Cassie, but he was actually looking forward to getting quality time alone with her. It was something he hardly ever got to do.

When he met back up with her in front of school, he noticed she had put on her FC Barcelona cap. She was the best girl soccer player her age in town, the way she was the best softball pitcher. And Lionel Messi was her favorite player. Cassie talked about Messi the way Teddy talked about Odell Beckham Jr.

"I've been thinking about something," Teddy said to her now. "Do you think you might already be taller than Messi?"

"Making fun of my guy," she said, "is not the way to go."

"Am I allowed to ask where we're going?"

"I thought we'd go sit up above the water at Small Falls," she said.

"And do what?"

"Talk about how you have to stop acting like an idiot about your father," she said.

"And what if I don't want to talk about my dad?" he said.

It made Cassie laugh. "Oh," she said, "you were being serious."

He shook his head. One of the great things about Cassie Bennett, one of the many great things, was that she could somehow be funny and cool and obnoxious all at the same time. And it was your job to keep up with her.

"Can't we just start talking about him now and get it out of the way?" Teddy said.

"No," she said.

They spent the rest of the walk talking about her soccer team and his football team and about the first week of school, and talking again about how they had to find a way to save Mrs. Brandon's job and the music department. The thought of the town closing down the department had upset Cassie the way it had Teddy's mom. Cassie didn't love music as much as she loved sports. But not only had she become a terrific piano player, despite all the complaining she did about having to *go* to piano lessons, she loved Mrs. Brandon.

"If they close the department, this will be her last year with us."

"And you're not going to let that happen," Teddy said.

"Not if I can help it."

"You know my mom feels the same way," Teddy said. "She's been trying to come up with a plan."

"Maybe we can all come up with a plan together," Cassie said. "We've got to find a way to raise enough money to save the department and save her job."

"Saving Mrs. B!" Teddy said.

"You better not think this is funny."

"I think it's great," Teddy said. "And whenever you do come up with something, I'm in."

"Let's be honest," Cassie said, grinning. "It's not like you really had a choice."

They finally got to Journey's End Road and made their way toward the water. When they got close, Cassie took off ahead of him, yelling, "Catch me if you can!"

Teddy ran hard after her, knowing there was no chance of ever really catching this girl, now or ever.

They sat halfway up the hill on this side of the water. The only noise up here, Teddy thought, *was* the water. It was like they had found their own private corner of the world.

"You have to stop acting like this," Cassie said. "Jack and Gus won't tell you that. Not saying stuff out loud is part of the boy code. But I will."

"Stop acting like what?" Teddy said. "Like I haven't figured out something I haven't figured out?"

"No, it's not that," she said. "You have to stop acting like your dad coming back is some kind of great tragedy. It's not. Jack's brother dying the way he did, *that's* a tragedy. Not this."

"You think I don't know the difference?" Teddy said.

"If you do, you're not acting like it," she said. "You haven't been acting anything like yourself lately."

"And how do I act like myself?" he said. "Do I have to get a Teddy app?"

"By being funny. The guy I wanted to be friends with was funny."

"You want me to tell more jokes?"

"This is no joke."

"I was trying to be funny Teddy."

"Well, it's not working," she said.

She stood up, picked up a rock, and tried to throw it as far as she could across the water. She nodded like she was satisfied with the throw, and sat back down. "You know what you're starting to do? You're starting to act as dumb as Jack did when he quit baseball to punish himself for his brother dying."

"Wait a minute!" Teddy said. "You were the one who told him not to play if he didn't want to play."

"Until I found out why he wasn't playing."

"You're right," Teddy said, because she was.

"I was right about him, and I'm right about you. You're still mad at him leaving, but you can't see that the worst part for you, the time you missed with him, is already over."

"And you figured this out all by yourself? Maybe when you become a TV star, it should be doing one of those shows like Dr. Phil."

It got a smile out of her. "My mom might have helped me with some of it," Cassie said. "My grandma and grandpa divorced when she was six. And guess what? She survived!"

"Did I ever say I'm not going to survive? You're acting as if I'm not just walking around underneath a dark cloud, I *am* the dark cloud."

"Whatever," she said. "You want to know my biggest problem with this whole thing? You've already made up your mind that you don't like the guy, forget about ever loving him."

"Not gonna happen."

"But you don't have any idea what he's like! You're the one who says the two of you have never talked. How about talking to him before you decide he's a jerk?"

"Not a jerk. An idiot."

"You know this . . . *how*?"

Teddy looked at her. "Because only an idiot would leave my mom."

He was the one who got up now, walked around until he found a good throwing stone, and cut loose.

"Good arm," she said.

"Thanks."

"You might have the best arm in our grade after Jack," she said, before adding, "Out of the guys."

"I'd rather catch."

"Even when you're catching heat from me?"

"I could've said no when you told me what you wanted to talk about," he said. "But I have found out, the hard way, that it's best for me to keep an open mind with you."

"So keep one with your dad!" she yelled.

He sat back down and looked down at the water. It was weird, he thought. It was like different water now that he wasn't afraid of it anymore.

"You're like that woman Mrs. Henson was quoting to us in English the other day," he said. "Often wrong, never uncertain."

"Well," she said, "the second part is right."

In her mind, she hardly ever *was* wrong. But he still liked being with her. He knew she was trying to be a good friend today. She was just doing it in her own way: by being a know-it-all. But the way she did it, with a smile, made it hard for Teddy to ever get really mad at her.

"You just like him because he told you how smart you were the other night, and that you were going to be on ESPN someday. I think I might have even seen some blushing after he did."

"Don't make me mad."

"You know what makes me really mad about him?" Teddy said. "That he acts like all he has to do is show up now and he gets all his dad privileges back. Like practically taking over the end of practice."

"Maybe it's just his way of trying."

"Or maybe he just thinks he's so cool he can win everybody over, including me."

"Maybe," Cassie said. "But you don't know that yet."

"I still think he's an idiot for leaving my mom and hurting her."

"Is that what this is about? Or that he left you? And hurt you?"

"And now I'm just supposed to let it all go, is that what you're saying?"

"Yup," she said. "Let . . . it . . . go."

"Are you ready to go?"

MIKE LUPICA

She jumped to her feet. "I am!"

"Before we go, can I ask you one serious question?" he said, trying to make his face serious.

"Sure," she said.

"If you do get on television, which Simpsons character do you think you'll be?"

This time she chased him.

NINE

I t was the morning of the first game of the season, and the first official game of Teddy's life, against the Hollis Hills Bears, eleven o'clock, Holzman Field.

Teddy had to stop himself from putting on his uniform before he went down to breakfast.

He had laid out everything neatly before he went to bed, everything except his number 13 jersey, which was hanging in his closet. His mother had washed his pants after practice on Thursday night, and they were draped over the reading chair next to his desk. His socks were on the chair too, and the gray "Wildcats" T-shirt he would wear under his jersey. His shoulder pads were on his desk.

Everything still looked brand-new. He hoped that none of the guys noticed he had even polished his black spikes.

His helmet was on the nightstand.

Teddy had been awake since six thirty but waited until eight to go downstairs, messing around on his laptop until then, trying to calm himself down, knowing how long it was until kickoff. There was always a lot of nervous excitement before big baseball games, especially once they'd made it to Williamsport and ESPN began televising them.

He knew those games, played in front of the whole country, should have made him more nervous. They hadn't. He liked baseball. But he had always wanted to be a football player, and today he finally was.

When he got to the kitchen, his mom was at the table, glasses at the end of her nose, reading the morning paper. She looked at him over the glasses and smiled.

"Any big plans today?" she said.

"I thought I'd start by cleaning out the garage," he said.

"Then move on to those boxes of my stuff in the basement you've been wanting me to sort through, before I do all my homework for the weekend."

"What about mowing the lawn?"

"Well," he said, "I thought I should save *something* for after lunch."

She asked him what he wanted to eat. He said just cereal; his stomach felt too jumpy to try anything heavier.

"I actually read that cereal and some yogurt is good for a football player before an early game," his mom said.

"You *heard*, Mom? Where?"

"I might have read something on the Internet."

"You always have been so curious about the dietary habits of football players."

She got out the milk and cereal, some yogurt, and a banana to go with the cereal. As she laid everything out she said, "So how are we looking?"

"I wasn't this scared on my first day of school," he said. "But Jack's always telling me this is a good kind of scared."

"You're going to do great."

"I would settle for not stinking up the place," he said. "Or not dropping a pass that would've won the game, or not fumbling. Or committing a dumb penalty."

She grinned. "Well, it's always good to think positively."

MIKE LUPICA

"Did I mention that I'm hoping not to run out on the field without my helmet?"

"You know, I heard some players call helmets 'hats,'" she said.

"Another thing you heard!" Teddy said. "Where this time, the gym?"

"You can find out a lot of interesting things about football on the Internet," she said. "I'm just putting that out there."

He ate in silence for a couple of minutes. She went back to reading the paper. When he finished eating, she said, "I haven't even asked—how are you planning to get to the game?"

"Jack said he could pick me up, if I wanted."

"Nope," she said. "I'll take you."

There was another silence at the table, before Teddy said, "Is he planning to come?"

They both knew who he was talking about.

"He said he was," Teddy's mom said.

"Figured," Teddy said. "You two going to sit together?"

"It doesn't matter whether we do or not," she said. "This isn't his day. It's not my day. It's yours. Just remember that."

Then she pointed at him, her face serious, and said, "And to wear your helmet."

She said she'd clean up. He went back upstairs, killed more time on his computer, texted Jack and Gus and Cassie. Finally it was a quarter to ten, and time for him and his mom to leave for the field. He put on his uniform and walked down the stairs, helmet in hand.

On his way through the front hall, he caught a glimpse of himself in the full-length mirror. Not knowing his mom was watching, he turned and took a better look.

"Looks like a football player to me," she said.

"Remember that time I dressed up like a player for Halloween?" Teddy said. "I almost just said 'trick or treat.'"

"Not today, number thirteen," she said. "Definitely not today."

TEN

Everything was in fast-forward from the time he got to the field.

He stretched with the rest of the Wildcats. He warmed up with Jack, along with the rest of the receivers. When he looked over to the stands, even they seemed to be filling up quickly, as if everybody at Holzman Field couldn't wait for the season to officially start.

Teddy noticed that his mom and dad were standing next to

each other, right in front of Mr. and Mrs. Callahan and Gus's parents.

I've finally got a dad in the stands, Teddy thought. *I just don't know how I really feel about that.*

Cassie was down near the field with some of her soccer teammates, standing in the narrow area between the fence behind the Wildcats' bench and the first row of the bleachers.

She waved Teddy and Jack and Gus over to her, maybe ten minutes before the kickoff.

"Well," she said to them, "this is what we've been waiting for."

"We?" Teddy said. He looked at Jack and Gus, who both shrugged.

"Behind every good man is a good woman," Cassie said. "Haven't you ever heard that one?"

"What if it's three men?" Gus said.

"Well, that would probably require a *great* woman, wouldn't it?"

Teddy looked past her, up into the stands. "If you spot a great woman at the game, let us know."

"I'd *definitely* like to meet somebody like that," Jack said.

"Okay, enough chitchat," she said. "Go make yourselves useful and win the game."

She knuckle-bumped them, one after another. Teddy was

last. Before he turned to leave, he couldn't help himself, as nervous as he was. He tipped back his helmet and smiled at her.

"You're ready," she said.

"You know what?" Teddy said. "I am."

For as long as Teddy had been a football fan, he'd heard announcers on NFL games talk about how much the game sped up when you went from college to the pros. Well, maybe the same thing happened when you went from never having played a real game of football to *here*.

The Wildcats won the coin toss and decided to take the ball. And once they were into their offense, Teddy was glad that Coach wanted them to start with all running plays, because that meant all he had to do to start was some basic blocking. Even with that, he felt like his heart was in a race with his brain as he tried to remember exactly where he was supposed to be.

On the Wildcats' fourth play from scrimmage, he forgot the snap count by the time he lined up next to Billy Curley, their huge offensive right tackle. But even though he had to wait a beat for Billy to come off the blocks, Teddy managed to put a solid block on the Bears' outside linebacker, cleaned him out so that Jake Mozdean could gain five extra yards.

Only when Jake ripped off another ten-yard run and the Wildcats were at the Bears' thirty-five yard line did Teddy feel as if he finally had a chance to catch his breath.

Just as Jack called for their first pass of the game.

To Teddy.

"Strong side curl," Jack said in the huddle. It meant Teddy and Gus would line up on the right side, Gus behind him in the slot. But once Gus broke from his spot, Teddy was supposed to wait and run behind him for about ten yards, then stop and turn, hopefully in a nice, empty soft spot in the Bears' defensive back field.

"Be ready," Jack said to Teddy as they came out of the huddle. "The ball might be headed your way before you turn."

"You throw, I'll catch," Teddy said.

Teddy told himself not to rush: the play was designed for him to look like a decoy, or at least a secondary receiver, until Gus made a hard cut to the outside. As soon as he did, Teddy took one more step and turned around.

Jack Callahan had *not* been lying. The pass—a bullet—was already on top of him, Jack having seen the safety closing from Teddy's right.

Teddy saw the kid coming but told himself to focus on the ball, even knowing he was going to get popped as soon as he caught it. He looked the ball all the way into his belly as it caught him right above his belt buckle, knocking the air out of him before the safety knocked him down.

But he held on and saw the ref closest to him signaling that it was a first down.

He was on the board.

On the way back to the huddle, he couldn't help himself. He looked up into the stands to where his mom and dad were. But he was only looking for his mom. It was as if she'd been waiting for him to look over there, because as soon as he did, she patted her heart twice, while Teddy saw his dad high-fiving Mr. Morales.

Teddy quickly patted his own heart, his hand there and gone, hoping she had noticed.

Three plays later the Wildcats scored their first touchdown of the season. Jack delivered another strike, this one to Gus Morales. Gus put a killer move on the cornerback covering him and broke free between the goal posts. It was 6–0.

The rules of their league were like a lot of Pop Warner leagues: You got two points on the conversion for a kick, just because there weren't a lot of good placekickers their age. You got one point if you ran it in or threw. Jack handed the ball to Jake, Teddy helped him by blasting the Bears' middle linebacker, and Jake went into the end zone untouched. It was 7–0, Wildcats.

"It's like you've been making catches like that your whole life," Coach Gilbert said when Teddy got to the sideline.

"I have," Teddy said. "Just in my dreams."

The Bears came right back with a drive of their own. Their quarterback didn't have the arm that Jack did, but he could throw well enough, and run it even better. He finally called a quarterback draw for himself for his team's first score and ran an option play to perfection on the conversion. It was 7-all.

"Boys," Gus said to the other guys on the offense, "I do believe a game just broke out here."

But then both defenses, almost acting insulted about the way the game had begun, dominated the first half from there. Teddy thought they might get to halftime with the score still 7–7 until Jack completed a couple of passes, one to Gus and one to Mike O'Keeffe, in the last two minutes.

They finally ended up at the Bears' twelve yard line, fourth-and-one, ten seconds left, the Wildcats out of time-outs.

At this point, Jack made the kind of play that star players just made in sports, out of the shotgun, the kind of play that can change everything.

And did.

As Jack called out the signals, he clapped his hands right before Charlie Lyons, their center, was supposed to snap him the ball. Jack was trying to get Gus's attention, wanting him to go in motion.

But when he clapped his hands, Charlie thought Jack wanted

the ball and snapped it, even though Jack's head was turned. The ball banged off Jack's shoulder pads, bouncing away from him, to his left.

At this point, the whole thing turned into the kind of play that Coach Gilbert liked to call a jailbreak.

Jack managed to get to the ball before the Bears' outside linebacker did, scooped it up, immediately reversed his field, and started running to his right. The play he'd called in the huddle was supposed to be a fade pass to Mike O'Keeffe in the right corner of the end zone, but *that* wasn't happening now.

Teddy was on the opposite side of the field from Jack, looking for open spaces while so much of the Bears' defense chased Jack.

Then he remembered something:

When in doubt, follow Jack Callahan.

He was still in the back field, trying to pick up blockers and get outside. Teddy was open by now, heading his way, waving his arm for the ball. But as he did, he saw that Jack was going to run for it.

He couldn't get to the sideline to stop the clock; the Bears had cut that off. And by now, even if he tried to throw the ball away, the half was probably going to be over by the time he did.

It meant Teddy was a blocker now, as soon as he could find somebody to block.

THE EXTRA YARD

He saw the Bears' middle linebacker sprinting from Jack's left as Jack cut toward the orange pylon. But Teddy didn't move quickly enough to cut him off or even get in his way.

He stopped and watched what happened next as if it were happening in slow motion.

He saw Jack dive for the pylon, extending the ball as he did, at the same moment the middle linebacker launched himself at him.

Saw the midair collision that knocked Jack sideways, even as he was trying to jam the ball down on the pylon before his body hit the ground, like a basketball player jamming home a dunk.

Saw Jack land hard on his right shoulder.

The ref's arms went straight up in the air, meaning touchdown, Wildcats.

But the Wildcats' quarterback was still down.

ELEVEN

Jack's parents were there right away. So was Coach Gilbert, and Coach Williams, and Dr. McAuley, Brian's dad, who served as the Wildcats' team doctor.

Teddy's dad was standing behind them.

"Same thing happened to me once," Teddy could hear him saying to Dr. McAuley. "It's like a fighter getting a free swing at a guy. You're defenseless."

Coach Gilbert had told all of Jack's teammates to stay back.

But none of them had stayed back very far. Teddy was closest to Jack, feeling like he wanted to cry. Or like he might be sick. If he had just been a step quicker, just that, he could have at least gotten between the linebacker and Jack.

Coach Gilbert and Coach Williams gently rolled Jack over so he was on his back. Jack's dad helped them, whispering something to his son as he did.

Teddy moved a couple of steps closer. He wanted to hear everything they were saying.

"Where does it hurt?" Dr. McAuley was saying now.

"Everywhere," Jack said.

"Back of the shoulder or front?"

"Both."

"Jack," Dr. McAuley said, "we're going to try to gently lift you so you can sit up."

They did that. Teddy looked at Jack's mom, whose eyes were very wide. Coach Gilbert took Jack's helmet off. Teddy could see the pain on Jack's face. Then Dr. McAuley was between Teddy and Jack, speaking quietly. Teddy saw Jack nodding. Then Dr. McAuley said something to Coach Williams, who ran back to the oversize first aid kit behind the bench that reminded Teddy more of a cooler and came back with a sling.

To Teddy, it already felt as if Jack had scored his touchdown an hour ago.

After Jack's arm was in the sling, he stood up. The people in the stands and players on both teams applauded as he walked slowly back toward the Wildcats' bench.

Once Jack and the adults with him were off the field, the refs motioned for both teams to line up for the conversion. Teddy took another look back at their bench and saw Danny Hayes, the backup quarterback, running onto the field, fastening his chin strap as he did. He knelt down, talking fast, told them the play was a fake to Jake and a pass in the left corner to Mike O'Keeffe. The pass fell way short of Mike and was nearly intercepted. It was still Wildcats 13, Bears 7 at the half.

By the time they came off the field, Jack was already on his way to the hospital for X-rays.

Coach Gilbert gathered the team around him right away.

"Listen," he said, "we all know this isn't the game we thought we were going to play. It might not even be the same season we thought it was going to be. We'll know more about that later."

They had made a big circle around him. Coach kept turning as he spoke, as a way of talking to all of them at once.

"But as great a player as Jack is, and I really believe he's a great player, one guy is never a team. And Danny here"—he pointed at Danny Hayes—"wouldn't be on this team if I didn't think he could do the job at quarterback."

Teddy could see some of the guys nodding their heads in

agreement, even though nobody had any idea how Danny was going to do in the second half.

"I'm not one of those guys who tries to tell you what somebody else would want," Coach said. "But I'm pretty doggone sure, knowing Jack the way I do, that he wouldn't want you to be worrying about him right now. I'm pretty sure he'd want us to go win this game."

Teddy could see him smiling. "And since we're all here, and there's still a whole half left to play, why don't we just go ahead and do that?"

But the Bears scored the second time they had the ball in the third quarter, after the cornerback covering Gus had intercepted the second pass Danny tried. Five plays later their quarterback found their tight end wide open in the end zone. The quarterback ran it in himself on the conversion, and the Bears were ahead 14–13.

As nervous as Teddy had been trying to make the Wildcats, Danny was even more nervous trying to replace Jack at quarterback. He nearly fumbled a couple of simple handoffs, one to Jake and one to Brian. And when he did try a couple of throws on their next drive, they didn't come close to connecting. Teddy wanted to tell him to relax, the way Jack was always telling him to relax. But he wasn't sure, in the first game he'd ever played, that it was his place, as much as he wanted to be a good teammate. On top of that, he barely knew Danny Hayes.

The first time Danny threw a ball Teddy's way, a simple slant pattern on the Wildcats' last drive of the third quarter, the ball was so far behind Teddy it nearly got picked by the cornerback covering Gus. The only reason the kid dropped the ball was because he seemed shocked it was anywhere close to him.

The Wildcats punted again. They held the Bears again, three and out. The Bears punted. Another three and out for the Wildcats, still down a point. And the deeper the game went into the fourth quarter, the bigger that point looked.

"We are *not* losing this game," Gus said to Teddy on the sideline as their defense tried to get them another stop and get the offense back on the field.

"You are aware," Teddy said, "that you said the exact same thing every time we were trailing in a baseball game?"

"Your point being?"

"Got nothing," Teddy said. "You're right. My point is that we're not letting that stupid point on the board stand up for those guys."

The Bears were deep into Wildcats territory by then. But on a third-and-three play at the twenty yard line, Max Conte fought off a couple of blocks, caught up with the Bears' quarterback just as he was getting to the edge, knocked the ball loose with his right hand, and recovered it.

Three minutes left. Eighty yards to go. No Jack. Right before Teddy ran back onto the field with the rest of the offense, he looked over and noticed that his dad was standing next to Coach Gilbert. And that his dad was doing most of the talking.

"What's he doing down here?" Teddy said.

"He was a quarterback, right?" Gus said. "Maybe he's our new quarterback coach."

Teddy's mom had said before the game that this wasn't about his dad. But maybe his dad thought everything was.

When they were all in the huddle, Danny said, "We're gonna pound it with Jake and Brian, and then try to move the ball with short passes." He looked around at his teammates and said, "Coaches figure even I can accurately throw a ball five yards."

Now Teddy spoke. "You throw," he said. "We'll catch."

Jake ran for eight yards. Brian ran for six. First down. But after the Bears stuffed Jake for no gain, Danny completed his first pass of the second half, a little dump-off throw to Gus in the flat. Gus dusted the linebacker closest to him with a great move and ran for twenty yards before one of the Bears' safeties knocked him out of bounds. Now the Wildcats were in Bears territory.

Under two minutes to go.

Jake, who had been a horse all day, ran straight up the middle for ten more yards. Danny completed another short pass, this one to Mike O'Keeffe. Right at the end of the play Teddy threw a huge block, and Mike gained five extra yards.

Just like that they were at the Bears' nineteen yard line.

Brian ran for five yards, couldn't get out of bounds.

Thirty-eight seconds left.

Coach called time-out. Teddy took another look up into the stands. He saw his mom on her feet with the rest of the Wildcats parents, her hands clasped in front of her, looking nervous and happy and excited all at the same time. It meant she felt pretty much the way he did right now.

He looked over at his dad now, couldn't help himself, saw him leaning forward, hands on his knees, looking as fierce as guys like Jim Harbaugh did on the sideline. Like he was coaching the team as much as Coach Gilbert was. Like he was the one calling the plays. Maybe he was.

Danny had run over to their bench during the time-out and came sprinting back to the huddle now.

"Tight end screen to Teddy," he said.

It was a play they hadn't run all day and really didn't run that often in practice. But one that required almost perfect timing, from Danny, from the blockers, from Teddy, who when the play started was supposed to look like a blocker himself.

Danny did his job perfectly, looking away from Teddy at first as the rush came up on him, then turning and throwing at the last second while the guys on the right side of the line and Jake had set up a wall of blockers.

The problem was that it was one of the worst throws of all time.

Danny, under pressure, had short-armed the ball. Teddy had done it himself his first few games in baseball, when he'd tried to throw out guys trying to steal second on him.

As the ball started to drop, Teddy thought he had no shot at it, that it was going to hit the ground, incomplete, play over. But somehow he managed to get to it in time and clearly get his big hands underneath it.

That was the good news.

Bad news?

The play had taken *way* too long to develop, and a whole bunch of defenders were about to be all over him. As Teddy turned back toward the line of scrimmage, so he could get himself going in the right direction, it looked like there were suddenly two Bears to every one Wildcats blocker.

But what the defenders from the Bears didn't know, because how could they, was how long Teddy Madden had waited for a moment like this.

He didn't know whether the first guy with a shot at him was a defensive tackle or linebacker. No time to check the guy's number. But Teddy thought, *Take a number, bud*. Teddy straight-armed the kid and broke to the outside at the same time.

The next kid tried to hit him high. It would have done the job once, with the old Teddy. But not now. Teddy shrugged off the hit and kept on going.

Somebody—Jake?—cleared out a linebacker. Teddy was at the ten yard line by now, Gus right ahead of him, trying to pick out one of the two guys in front of him to block.

Wait for it, Teddy told himself.

Gus took the kid on the outside. Teddy broke to the inside, seeing the Bears' safety with a clear path to him, thinking he had Teddy lined up.

And he did.

He came in low with his front shoulder, catching Teddy above the knees. It should have made for a good, solid tackle.

Except it wasn't a tackle if the guy with the ball wouldn't go down. Teddy Madden wouldn't go down.

Somehow he kept his legs driving. The safety had grabbed hold of Teddy's right leg. Still Teddy wouldn't go down, dragging the kid along with him toward the goal line.

He was at the two or three by now, feeling himself start to fall, taking one more giant step and reaching out with his right hand as he did, the ball firmly in his grip; reaching out the way his man Beckham did with his own big hands sometimes.

Right before either of his knees touched the ground, the ball crossed the plane, he was sure of it.

The ref was right in front of Teddy, yelling "Touchdown!" even before he got his arms up in the air.

Wildcats 19, Bears 14.

Teddy just got up and handed the ball to the ref, even though he wanted to do one of those Rob Gronkowski spikes. He let his teammates pound on him briefly, before they all collected themselves and lined up for the conversion. The guys on the O-line blew everybody off the ball, and Brian could have walked the ball into the end zone.

Wildcats 20, Bears 14.

The guys on defense knocked down four straight desperation passes from the Bears' quarterback, and it was over.

David Madden came running down the sideline, got in front of Teddy, grabbed him by his shoulder pads, and yelled, "Was that a great call from your old man, or what?"

TWELVE

Teddy just said, "Yeah, great call," to his dad, even though he was amazed that his father would rather talk about the play call than the play Teddy had made.

Then Teddy broke away from him and walked over to where his mom was standing. As happy as she'd looked watching the game, she looked even happier now, like one of her favorite expressions: over the moon.

"Can't we just call it a season right here?" she said after she'd hugged him, not caring about the dirt on the front of his uniform.

"Pretty sure we'll keep going," he said.

"Like you kept going with half the town of Hollis Hills trying to tackle you?"

"Coach always tells us that if you keep your legs moving, good things will happen in football."

"Or great things."

"Not so great about Jack," Teddy said. "Have you heard anything about how he's doing?"

His mom turned Teddy slightly and pointed. "Why don't you go ask him yourself?"

Jack was behind the Wildcats' bench with his mom and dad, Mr. and Mrs. Morales, Cassie, and Gus. Jack had a different sling on, one that looked bigger and stronger than the one Dr. McAuley had put on after the injury. Teddy ran over to him, but when he got close, Jack grinned and put up his left arm, even being careful with that one.

"Slow down," he said. "You already scored."

"You saw?"

"I got back just in time," Jack said. "It was like a play I saw once on NFL Films, Mark Bavaro, an old Giants tight end, practically carrying the whole 49ers defense on his back."

Teddy knew the play too. He loved looking up stuff on the

old teams that had won the Giants' first Super Bowls. He had always liked history in school, but he liked Giants history most of all.

"Forget about me," Teddy said. "How are you?"

"Separated shoulder," Cassie said. "Grade two."

Teddy grinned at her. "Thanks for the diagnosis, Dr. Bennett."

"You didn't specify that Jack had to be the one who answered," Cassie said.

"Let her have her fun," Jack said. "You know how obsessed she is with having the right answer in class."

"Separated shoulder doesn't sound like much fun," Teddy said.

"Doc said it could have been worse," Jack said. "For now he's saying eight weeks. Six, if I'm a fast healer."

Teddy said, "I should have been faster putting a body on the guy who hit you."

"Stop," Jack said. "It's a contact sport. Stuff happens."

"It shouldn't have happened to you in the first half of the first game of the season."

"We'll be fine," Jack said. "We won, didn't we?"

"Barely," Teddy said. "How much does it hurt?"

"Little bit if I'm careful, a lot if I try to make any kind of move with my right arm," Jack said. "Doc told me to start learning how to be a one-handed typist, and to brush my teeth with my left hand."

"You brush?" Cassie said.

"This stinks," Teddy said. "Totally."

"Dude," Jack said. "I'll survive. And you get to be happy. You just won the game for us. And Gus says it was your dad who sent the play in."

Teddy looked out at the field and saw his dad throw another high five Coach Gilbert's way.

"Yeah," Teddy said. "Maybe we should give him the game ball."

"But they're giving it to you, right?" Cassie said.

"*Cassie!*" Jack and Gus shouted at the same time.

"He doesn't know?"

Jack and Gus slowly shook their heads.

Cassie said, "Well, the next time something is a secret, maybe one of you two could tell me that."

Coach Gilbert yelled at his players then, waving them out to where he'd been standing with David Madden. When they got around him, the first thing he did was present Teddy with the ball he'd been holding.

"It's always the same in sports," Coach said. "You make a play or you don't. And you made one when we needed one today."

Teddy thanked Coach Gilbert and said, "It feels a little light. You didn't take any air out of it, did you?"

Coach was a Patriots fan and was still taking heat for that time when the Patriots had been accused of taking air out of their game balls in an AFC Championship game.

"Just how long are you guys gonna make fun of me about Deflategate?" he said.

"Only when we're not making fun of you for the two Super Bowls the Giants got off you," Teddy said.

"Thanks a bunch," Coach said.

The guys laughed and pounded on Teddy a little more. When he broke away from them, he walked back over to Jack and tried to hand him the ball.

"This is yours," he said.

"Don't even think about it," Jack said, taking a step back. "It's all you."

"Okay, I'm not gonna fight you. Even though I'm pretty sure I could take you right now."

Teddy didn't even notice that his dad had joined them.

"You know what wasn't a fair fight?" David Madden said. "Two of them against you."

"Thanks," Teddy said.

He felt himself getting annoyed all over again, like his dad had joined a party that Teddy hadn't invited him to. But it was

THE EXTRA YARD

clear now that there was nothing to do about it. And that his dad wouldn't be leaving the party anytime soon.

Jack said he had to go home, his parents wanted him to rest. But he said for Teddy and Gus and Cassie to check with him later—maybe they could all come over.

Teddy went and collected the big bag he'd brought with him to the game, put his helmet and the game ball inside it, walked past the bleachers, and started to make the turn for the parking lot. Before he did, though, he took one last look back at the field.

Wow, he thought.

Wow, wow, wow.

What a day.

When he got to his mom's car, she said, "Where's the ball?" As if he'd lost it.

"In the bag."

"We're going to need a trophy case!" she said.

"Okay, Mrs. Madden," he said. "Let's put the brakes on here."

"Got carried away there, didn't I?"

"Little bit."

When they were both in the car, they saw Coach Gilbert and David Madden heading into the parking lot, arms around each other's shoulders. Teddy imagined they'd left a lot of fields in their lives the same way.

Teddy's mom said, "He really seemed to enjoy himself today."

"Gee, I hadn't picked up on that."

"Let's face it, honey," she said. "This is all new to him, too. He's just trying to figure things out the way the rest of us are."

"Now you're defending him?" Teddy said.

"Not defending him. Just looking out for you."

"By defending him?"

"No," she said. "By telling you that you can't let everything he does get under your skin. If you do, you're going to be angry every time he's around. And you're going to have to deal with the fact that he's going to be around."

"I'm not angry."

"Really," she said.

He turned to face her in the front seat. "You're saying I don't have a right to be at least a little sketched out now that he's barged his way onto my team the way he barged his way back into our life?"

"Honey," she said. "I get it. I do. But you've got to get past being angrier now that he's back than you ever were when he was away."

Teddy slumped back into his seat as she put the car into gear.

"Just because Coach is letting him call some plays doesn't mean he gets to call all of them."

"Tell him that the next time you're alone," she said. "But right now, we're going to go home and you're going to clean up, and then you're going to enjoy the rest of the day with your friends. You did win today, remember?"

"Did I?" Teddy said.

THIRTEEN

His dad showed up for two of the three practices before their next game, on the road, against the Moran Mustangs. The only one he missed started too early for him to get there from his job.

Teddy just accepted it as being part of what Cassie liked to call his "new normal," knowing there was nothing he could do to stop his father from becoming more and more involved with the team. If Coach Gilbert wanted him as an assistant coach—it was what he'd become, even if nobody was calling him Coach Madden yet—it wasn't as if Teddy could do anything to change his mind.

And as much as Teddy hated admitting it, even to himself, his dad knew his football. It turned out Coach Gilbert had been right when he'd said that his old quarterback saw things on the field that nobody else did, sometimes before they even happened.

"I know you probably don't want to hear what I have to say," Gus said during a water break at Thursday night's practice, "but I'm going to say it anyway."

"What if I tell you that I not only don't want to hear it, but I really *don't* want you to say it?" Teddy said. "Think of all the trouble that might save both of us."

"But you don't know what it is yet."

"Just making what they call an educated guess."

"Meaning I've said things before that you didn't want to hear, but I said them anyway."

"Yes!"

Gus looked like he was trying not to laugh, but did.

"Anyway, here goes," he said.

"Has anybody ever told you that listening is not one of your strong suits?"

"I'm not listening," Gus said. "But what I'm trying to tell

you is that your dad is making us better, whether you like it or not."

"I don't like it."

"Him making us better?"

"No," Teddy said. "Him being around."

"Wow," Gus Morales said. "I hadn't picked up on that."

Coach blew his whistle, letting them all know the break was over. As they walked back to the field, Teddy said in a voice only loud enough for Gus to hear, "Listen, I can deal with having my dad around. But can we deal with having Danny be our quarterback?"

"Dude," Gus said, keeping his own voice low, always a struggle. "I hear you."

Teddy didn't know enough about Danny Hayes to know if he'd ever been a good quarterback in organized football before this. And he *had* been good enough to make the team as Jack's backup, no doubt. But the way he'd thrown the ball last Saturday and the way he'd been throwing it all week in practice made Teddy—and Gus, and Jack, who'd come to the two previous practices—wonder if he couldn't deal with the pressure of being the starter.

He wondered at the same time if Danny just couldn't think of himself as anything other than a backup.

Teddy knew something about that from his own life. His old

self. If you thought of yourself in a certain way long enough—the way Teddy used to think of himself as the funny, out-of-shape loser—you finally just became that kid.

But whatever was going on inside Danny's head, and maybe in his heart, the harder he tried, the worse his control got. Every time he dropped back to pass—in practice—it was as if the whole season were riding on his next completion.

Teddy and Gus and the rest of the players waited while Coach Gilbert, Coach Williams, and Teddy's dad huddled up, deciding how they wanted to scrimmage tonight.

"He was throwing spirals in tryouts," Teddy said. "I saw him. Now he can't even do that."

Gus said, "He's aiming every ball, even when he checks down to me or one of the backs. I feel bad for the guy."

"Me too," Teddy said. Now he was whispering. "But if this is as good as he can do, what are *we* gonna do?"

"Punt?" Gus said.

The coaches decided that they'd have a short scrimmage to end practice, the offense starting at the defense's thirty yard line. If they scored, the defense had to run two laps around the outside of Holzman Field.

If the defense could keep them out of the end zone, the guys on offense had to run.

After six plays, it all came down to fourth-and-goal from the nine. Danny hadn't completed a single pass to get them there, missing throws to both Gus and Teddy when they were both wide open. But the O-line had been terrific, opening up big holes for Jake and Brian, and Danny had managed to scramble for one of their first downs.

Now Coach Gilbert—or maybe Coach David Madden—called for the same screen to Teddy they'd used to beat Hollis Hills.

Only this time the throw was even worse than it had been against the Bears. This time Danny's pass floated into the flat, hanging in the air like a beach ball.

Andre Williams, coming from outside linebacker, read the play the whole way, seeing what Teddy did, that Danny had been eyeballing him from the time he got the snap in the shotgun. Teddy had no chance to cut him off; Andre was at full speed when he picked the ball off and ran ninety yards the other way.

Teddy chased him all the way, but as fast as he was, Andre was faster. He would have been better off saving his strength for the laps he was about to run.

When he and the rest of the guys from the offense finished, his dad came over to him and said, "This might not be the perfect moment to ask, but you want to grab a burger after you get cleaned up? When I talked to your mom, she said she hadn't even started dinner yet."

Teddy was sitting on the grass, gassed. He looked up at his dad and said, "You're gonna think I'm blowing you off."

"You mean like the other time when I asked and you blew me off?" his dad said, smiling as he did.

He *had* asked, the day after the Hollis Hills game, but Teddy already had plans to eat at Jack's house that night.

"It's just that I promised Cassie that I'd study with her for a history test tonight," Teddy said. "I just forgot to tell Mom."

He had to hand it to his dad. It was hard to knock that smile off his face. "Next time, then," he said. "Just wanted to talk a little bit about the team with you."

"Next time for sure!" Teddy said, trying to make himself sound a lot more fired up about the prospect than he actually was.

As soon as his dad was out of earshot, Teddy grabbed his phone out of his equipment bag and called Cassie. Of course she picked up right away.

"We're studying for history tonight at my house, okay? Half an hour?"

"You don't need my help with history."

"Just your help," Teddy said. "I told my dad I couldn't have dinner with him because we had to study."

"Loser."

"I just look at it as calling an audible," he said.

"See you in a few," she said, quickly throwing one more "loser" at him before she hung up.

Gus's mom dropped Teddy off, and he had enough time for a quick shower and a plate of pasta with his mom before Cassie showed up on her bike. When they were in his room, they didn't talk about school right away, or the test. Teddy told her what had happened with the team all week, how badly Danny was playing, how practice had ended tonight with Andre's pick six.

When he finished, Cassie looked at him and said, "You should play quarterback."

FOURTEEN

Teddy laughed, but then noticed that the expression on her face hadn't changed.

"Oh," he said, "you're serious."

She nodded her head slowly.

"You'll need to leave now," he said. "Studying with someone whose brain has stopped functioning does me no good."

Cassie stood up. "Get your football," she said. "There's still enough daylight for us to go over to school and play catch."

She got up and walked out of his room. Teddy grabbed his football from his closet and followed her, saying, "You do remember that I just finished practice and then had to run laps after practice and might be a little footballed out?"

"Maybe I should have said I was Teddy-ed out when you called me," she said as she headed out his back door. "Do you get my meaning?"

"Yes, ma'am."

"How many times do I have to tell you not to ma'am me?" she said. "I'm not your mother."

"Even if you act that way sometimes," he said under his breath.

"I heard that."

And then they both heard Jack Callahan say, "Even I heard it."

There he was, standing on the home-run side of the outfield fence, arm in his sling, smiling at both of them.

"You just happened to wander by?" Teddy said.

"She texted me and told me I had to come," Jack said. "What would you have done?"

"Run," Teddy said. "So you're in on her little plan too?"

"All in," Jack said. "I wish I'd thought of it first."

"Don't beat yourself up," Cassie said. "I never know when these genius thoughts are coming to me. And when they do, I can't stop them."

"It's best that you don't try," Teddy said.

Cassie had been right about the light; there was enough of it left, in the cool of the early evening, for them to play catch. It was actually Teddy's favorite time of the day to do it.

"Okay," Cassie said after they'd soft-tossed to warm up. "Tonight I'm the receiver, which I would be good enough to be on your fancy-pants team if I wanted to be. And you're the quarterback."

"How many times do I have to tell you? I'm a tight end, not a quarterback!"

Jack had come through the door in centerfield and was standing with them.

Teddy turned to him, "Help me out here."

"That's what we're trying to do."

"I've seen your arm," Cassie said. "I saw it in baseball, and I saw it the other day when you were chucking rocks at Small Falls. You *are* a quarterback. You just don't know it. Yet."

Teddy sighed. "That burger with my dad is suddenly sounding better and better." He turned back to Jack. "And I thought you were supposed to be my wingman."

Jack shrugged and patted his injured shoulder. "Maybe a bad wing turns you into a bad wingman," he said.

"Good one," Teddy said.

"Are we gonna do this before it starts to get dark or not?"

Cassie said. "And we're not here to talk about your dad tonight. We're here to talk about you."

"Don't you mean talk *at* me?"

They were about twenty yards apart by now. She whipped a hard pass at him that would have hit him right in the face if he hadn't gotten his hands up. "Have it your way," she said.

Teddy wondered what would have happened if she'd tried out for the Wildcats. He already knew how fast she was from watching her run the bases for her softball team. And he knew she could catch from the times she'd shown up on this field when Jack and Gus and Teddy were goofing around.

But when she started running real patterns now, which Teddy would call out to her, inside cuts or outside cuts or fly patterns down an imaginary sideline, she just looked like a football player, with hands and moves and the ability to look like a streak of light when she really turned it on.

They had been at it for about twenty minutes when Jack told Teddy to have her run a deep post.

"Let's see how accurate you are when you really air it out," Jack said.

"You want to see if I can be as accurate as *you* are."

"Just cut it loose," Jack said.

Teddy yelled at Cassie and told her what he wanted her to run. "I *know* what a deep post is," she yelled back. Then she took off, flying across the outfield grass before she broke off a sharp cut and angled toward the infield. She caught the ball in stride and kept running all the way to the pitcher's mound before she spiked the ball like a champion.

She picked up the ball and jogged back to where Teddy and Jack were waiting for her near the right-field wall. Cassie said, "You can throw it a mile. And you almost always hit what you're aiming at. And that, my friend, is what real quarterbacks do."

"Yeah," Teddy said, "I did that on a baseball field after supper, throwing to a—"

"Uh-oh," Jack said.

Even though Teddy hadn't finished his thought, he knew he was in trouble. He saw Cassie's eyes narrow to slits. "I am going to pretend I didn't hear what I almost just heard," she said.

Teddy grinned. "What I was about to say was that I was throwing to a gifted wide receiver who'd make anybody throwing to her look good."

"You're not him," she said, jerking her head in Jack's direction. "But you could do this."

"We already have a quarterback."

"No," Jack said, "we don't."

Teddy asked if they were done. Cassie said of course they were done, she'd proven her point, and her parents wanted her home before it started to get really dark. They walked through the door in the outfield fence and through Teddy's backyard and around to the front of the house, where she'd left her bike. Jack had called his mom, and she was on her way over to pick him up.

"This is crazy talk," Teddy said to Cassie, "even for you."

"Not if you want to win," she said.

Then she hopped on her bike and sped away down Teddy's street. As she was about to turn the corner and disappear, she yelled one more thing over her shoulder.

"Maybe being a QB runs in the family!"

Then she was gone.

"She does like to get the last word," Jack said.

"So I'm not allowed to say no to her?"

"I haven't found a way to yet," Jack said.

"What if I ask Coach to play quarterback and then I can't do it?"

"You mean like you couldn't play catcher, and you couldn't make the football team?" Jack said.

Teddy shook his head. "Forgot who I was talking to for a second."

Gail Callahan pulled up in her car. Jack said they could talk about this more tomorrow, before practice. But he told Teddy to think about what was best for the team. And what was best for the Wildcats was him at least taking a shot at being their quarterback.

"You really want some advice?" Jack said when he got to his mom's car.

"Whatever you got."

"Go ice your arm," Jack said. "We may need it on Saturday against Moran."

FIFTEEN

By the end of the first quarter it was 13–0 for the Moran Mustangs. It wasn't all Danny Hayes's fault. But it was mostly his fault.

He had thrown an interception that led to the first Mustangs score. When he had the Wildcats driving the next time they had the ball, he got hit hard from both sides at the end of a nice scramble. The ball popped straight up into the air and into the hands of the Mustangs' middle linebacker, who ran sixty yards for a touchdown. The play turned around so quickly that Teddy, even chasing the play as hard as he could, was still fifteen yards behind the kid when he crossed the goal line.

When Teddy and Gus got back to their bench area, Gus said, "We're going to lose 50–0 the way things are going."

Teddy's head whipped around, just to make sure Danny Hayes wasn't close enough to have heard. But he saw that Danny had already taken a seat at the end of the bench, where Coach Gilbert was kneeling and talking quietly to him.

"He's got to get better," Teddy said.

Max Conte had walked over to join them. "He can't get any worse."

Gus, keeping his voice down, said, "Listen, this has nothing to do with what kind of guy he is. We all know he's a great guy. But he's not a quarterback. At least not on this team."

Andre Williams, Coach Williams's son, had told them during the week that Coach Gilbert had talked to his dad about bringing Bruce Kalb, the other kid who'd tried out for quarterback, up from Pop Warner. But they'd decided, at least for now, to leave Bruce where he was and just trust that Danny would figure things out. While he did, they were going to have Jake Mozdean be their backup quarterback.

Only Danny wasn't figuring things out. He *was* getting worse instead of better.

"Maybe they'll put Jake in," Teddy said.

From behind them they heard Jake say, "But Jake doesn't want to go in. Jake wants to stay at halfback, where he belongs."

Teddy turned around. "I hear you," he said.

He looked up into the bleachers behind Jake on their side of the field. Moran was more than an hour away from Walton, but most of the parents had still made the trip. Even though Jack was hurt, Mr. and Mrs. Callahan had still driven him here. They were in the top row, along with Gus's parents and Teddy's mom. His dad had been standing next to Coach Gilbert from the start of the game. Now he was sitting next to Danny on the bench, an arm around his shoulder, clearly trying to give him a pep talk.

Teddy hoped it was a good one. After Danny had thrown his interception, Teddy had said to him, "You'll play your way through this."

Danny, head down, said, "It'll be basketball season by the time I do."

Right before the half, Danny seemed to find himself, completing a couple of short passes, one to Teddy, one to Gus. But mostly the 'Cats were running the ball, nothing fancy, almost all off-tackle stuff for Jake and Brian. The only time they ran wide, it was a little pitch to Gus that he nearly broke for a touchdown, but he was tripped up from behind by one of the Mustangs' outside linebackers.

But with thirty seconds left and the Wildcats with a third-and-goal at the Mustangs' eight, Danny rolled to his right to escape pressure from a blitz. But instead of just throwing the ball away, as he was taught to do near the goal line, he stopped and just flung the ball across the field in Gus's general direction.

And got intercepted again.

Of all the bad balls he'd thrown so far, this was by far the worst. The Mustangs' quarterback took a knee, and that was the end of the half.

When Danny got back to the bench along with the rest of the guys on offense, Coach Gilbert spoke to him again, and then turned and told Jake to start warming up. Jake nodded his head.

But as soon as Coach turned away, Jake looked at Teddy and shook his head before grabbing a ball and waving Gus to soft-toss with him.

Jack was standing behind the bench. He waved Teddy over to him.

"Now or never," Jack said.

"In the middle of the game? Without having taken any snaps at practice?"

"We should be out of this game already," Jack said. "But we're not. We can still win. If you don't want to ask Coach, ask your dad what he thinks."

"That would be a first."

"Go," Jack said.

Teddy took a deep breath, walked past where Jake was throwing with Gus, and walked around the bench, to where his dad was flipping through the pages of Coach Gilbert's playbook.

"Talk to you for a second?" Teddy said.

His dad stopped what he was doing, a surprised look on his face. Once the game had started, they hadn't talked at all. But then they hardly spoke at practice, either.

"What's on your mind?"

"We're gonna start Jake at QB in the second half?"

"Looks like. Dick—Coach Gilbert thinks the best thing for Danny, and for the team, is if he watches for a little bit."

Teddy took another deep breath, like he wanted to swallow up all the air around them before he said what he was about to say.

"Put me in," he said.

"Really?" his dad said.

"Really," Teddy said. "I've been practicing on my own, just in case. I can do this."

• • •

Teddy's dad walked over to Coach Gilbert and told him what Teddy had just suggested.

"You want to play quarterback?" Coach said.

"I didn't say I wanted to, Coach," Teddy said. "I just told my dad that I think I can."

Coach Gilbert turned and looked at the scoreboard clock. There were just under five minutes left before the second half started. He turned back to Teddy.

"It's one thing to know what you're supposed to do on a given play," he said. "Where you're supposed to be. It's another to know where everybody's supposed to be."

"But that's the thing. I do."

"You do."

"I learned the playbook the way Jack did," he said. "I do know where everybody's supposed to be and what they're supposed to do."

Coach stared at Teddy. He looked at David Madden, who smiled and shrugged. Coach said to Teddy, "You think you can do this."

"Here's what I know," Teddy said, knowing there was no turning back now, and knowing they were running out of time. "I know that Jake doesn't want to play quarterback. I know we're better off with him at halfback. So we'd be hurting two positions by moving him."

"It makes sense," Teddy's dad said. "He must get his common sense from his mother."

"Teddy," Coach said, "we all know by now you can catch it. But can you throw it?"

"Oh, he can throw it," Jack Callahan said. "Coach, you gotta trust me on this. I saw him throw out guys in baseball after he hadn't ever really played baseball. He can play quarterback even if he's never played quarterback."

Nobody said anything. Now Teddy checked the clock. Two minutes until the second half.

Finally Coach Gilbert laughed. "Why not?" he said. "Why the heck not? Teddy, go take the ball away from Jake and warm up. *Quickly.*"

Teddy said to Jack, "You want to hang around down here?"

"I've got nowhere else to be," Jack said.

Teddy ran down and said to Gus, "I'm going in at quarterback."

"Are you buggin'?" Gus said.

"Nope."

"*Word!*" Gus said.

He did warm up his arm as quickly as he could, putting some zip on the last few throws. Then Charlie Lyons came over, Teddy got behind him, and Charlie snapped the ball to him five or six times. When they finished, and the Wildcats and the

Mustangs were lining up for the second-half kick, Teddy said to Jack, "I actually feel pretty good."

"When you get out there, don't think the first time you throw. Just let it go."

"Thinking not always being my strong suit in sports?"

"Comes and goes," Jack said, and then carefully put out his left fist so Teddy could bump it.

The Wildcats were receiving. Teddy could feel his heart inside his chest like it was somebody beating on a door. When the ball was in the air, his dad came over and stood next to him.

"I can help you," he said.

Teddy tried to swallow, couldn't. His throat was that dry. "I know."

"So you'll let me?"

"Yes," Teddy said.

There was a huge cheer from the Wildcats fans as Jake Mozdean returned the second-half kickoff to midfield, giving them great field position.

"Just remember when you get out there," his dad said. "Don't pull back from center without the ball securely in those big hands. Don't leave it on the ground. Just turn and hand it to Jake on first down and get out of the way."

"Got it."

"You're playing the most fun position in sports," David Madden said. "Go have some fun."

"This is fun?" Teddy said.

He sprinted toward the huddle, thinking Jack had been right, as usual.

Now or never.

SIXTEEN

Teddy handled the first snap from Charlie just fine, but then nearly fumbled the ball when he handed it off to Jake, way too high with the ball, almost hitting Jake in his right shoulder pad.

Jake managed to hold on but was dropped for a two-yard loss. It was second-and-twelve. Brian came in with the play.

"Slot screen right," he said.

It was a short pass to Gus. Mike O'Keeffe, in for Teddy now

at tight end, was supposed to get out in front of Gus as quickly as he could, briefly screening the kid covering Gus. It couldn't be a block, and Mike had to act like a receiver running out on a pattern so that the refs wouldn't call an illegal pick. What Mike could do was become a blocker as soon as Gus caught the ball, if he did.

Teddy had seen Jack successfully run the play in practice plenty of times: straighten, turn, throw.

Teddy didn't baby the throw at all. He trusted it, the way Jack had told him to. He probably threw the ball harder than he needed to, not taking any chances that the first pass attempt of his life would be picked off. But Gus caught it. Mike threw a good block. So did Brian, busting it out of the backfield. Gus ran for fifteen yards and a first down.

As Gus ran back to the huddle, Teddy found his mom's face in the stands. She put up her fist. Teddy did the same. He was one-for-one.

The rest of the drive was like a roller coaster ride. Two plays later he did pull away too quickly from Charlie, in too much of a rush to drop back to pass, leaving the ball on the ground. He managed to fall on it right before the Mustangs' nose tackle did. But Jake cleaned that up for him on the next play, running for twelve yards on a quick pitch. Teddy hit Mike on a curl after that. Coach Gilbert—or maybe it was Coach Madden—called for a post pattern, wanting to go for a touchdown right here. Teddy never came close to getting the pass away, buried by a blitzing linebacker. But he held on to the ball.

They finally ended up with first-and-goal at the two. Teddy was sure they'd just give it to Jake and have him pound it in from there. But when Jake came in with the play, Teddy nearly laughed.

"Really?" Teddy said.

"I'm just the messenger," Jake said.

"Let's do this."

He pulled away from center, put the ball in Jake's gut, then took it out as Jake plowed into the line, bent over, like he still had the ball. Only Teddy had the ball on his hip, the way his dad had shown Jack how to hide it. Naked bootleg. Touchdown. This time he looked over at his dad, who shrugged and held out his hands, as if he hadn't been able to help himself.

I'll go back to being angry at him later, Teddy thought.

For now they had a game they were trying to come back and win.

Brian got to the outside for the conversion. It was 13–7. They were on the board. Coach Gilbert had been right. It wasn't the season any of them had expected.

But it sure wasn't dull.

• • •

The story of the game for the Wildcats for the rest of the third quarter and into the fourth was the way their defense was playing, doing everything it could to give the offense a chance to take the lead.

Teddy was totally clueless about how good the rest of the league was. He didn't know if Moran was one of the best teams or one of the worst, or how much an early-season loss would hurt them later on. But he couldn't worry about games they were going to play later. He just wanted to win this one. He wanted to see if he could actually be the kind of quarterback, even in his first shot at it, who could bring his team back from being two touchdowns behind and win.

He'd been intercepted once, at the end of the third quarter, trusting his arm *too* much, trying to squeeze a ball in to Mike O'Keeffe between two defenders. Their safety cut in front of Mike and picked the ball off. But then the Mustangs fumbled the ball right back to the Wildcats three plays later.

On the sideline his dad said, "Sometimes the smartest decision a quarterback makes all day is eating the ball."

"I've been telling myself not to overthink this deal," Teddy said. "That time I underthought."

"Welcome to the club, kid," he said. "There isn't a quarterback alive who hasn't done the same thing, no matter how long he's played the position."

Jack had stayed on the sidelines, as Teddy had asked him to do. He had tried to stay out of the way, especially when Coach Gilbert and Teddy's dad were talking to Teddy. It was as if Jack knew enough not to give Teddy too much information. Teddy told him at one point that he was afraid his brain might be running out of storage space the way his laptop did.

But before Teddy went back on the field, Jack got with him and said, "If you get a chance, take a shot down the field with Gus. That kid can't cover him deep."

"I've been a QB for about twenty seconds and now you want me to call an *audible*?"

"Are you kidding?" Jack said, shoving Teddy toward the field with his left hand. "This whole thing is an audible!"

It didn't happen on that series because the Wildcats went three and out, Teddy overthrowing Brian badly on third down. They punted the ball back to the Mustangs, who went three and out themselves and punted the ball back.

Four minutes left in the game. The Wildcats were still down 13–7.

On the sideline David Madden said, "Okay, here's what I think we should do."

"Dad," Teddy said. "Just send in the plays, okay? This isn't English class. I don't need an outline."

David Madden gave him a long look. "You're never easy, are you?"

"I'm me," Teddy said.

David Madden gave him another long look. "I'm good with that."

"Good."

Both teams were tired. It had been that kind of game. But the guys doing the grunt work for the Wildcats, the big boys in the offensive line, seemed less tired than everybody else on the field. They started opening up huge holes for Jake and Brian, so there was no need for Teddy to put the ball in the air. He was happy to keep handing off the ball as he kept an eye on the clock.

He wasn't out here to play a hero game. He just wanted to win. Somebody, probably Jack, had once said that a quarterback was like a point guard in basketball. The only stat that mattered was the final score.

After making five and six and seven yards a pop, the Wildcats finally stalled at the Mustangs' thirty, just under two minutes to go. As Jake Mozdean came running in with the next play, Gus said to Teddy, "I can beat my guy."

"I know."

"Let's go for it."

"Let's see what the play is."

It was a pass, just not to Gus. Nate Vinton had replaced Mike O'Keeffe at wide receiver after Mike moved over to tight end. The play was called "wideout chains." It simply meant that the intended receiver, Nate in this case, was to make a cut toward the sideline, and just make sure he was past the first-down markers.

But as Teddy and Gus broke the huddle together, Teddy whispered to him, "Take off."

Teddy was in the shotgun. Charlie Lyons gave him an easy snap to handle. Teddy made sure to eyeball Nate the whole way. It would have been a major quarterbacking sin if he was throwing to Nate.

Only he wasn't.

He'd called an audible.

He made a sweet pump fake to Nate, then turned and saw that Gus was streaking down the other side of the field, having beaten his man by five yards.

Teddy told himself to trust his arm as he let the ball go. His arm hadn't let him down so far, even when he'd been picked off.

His arm let him down now.

Gus Morales did not.

The ball was underthrown, badly. Teddy had put too much air under it when he saw how open Gus was. He could see it coming down short and behind Gus, like a terrible version of a back-shoulder throw. But Gus turned for the ball before the cornerback covering him did. He was able to put on the brakes and come back on the ball and somehow gather it in at the nine yard line before being knocked out of bounds.

"Dude!" Gus said when he got back to the huddle, as if that described everything that had just happened. With Gus, that one word, "dude," could be like a whole speech.

First-and-goal. Teddy didn't even look over at his dad, or Coach Gilbert. He didn't want to see their reaction to him having changed the play they'd sent in.

But all Brian said in the huddle when he brought in the next play was, "Coach Gilbert said that if you're that determined to have your buddy win the game, let's actually give him a chance to win it."

"That would be me," Gus said.

"Slot reverse," Brian said.

"Love it," Teddy Madden said.

He got under center, took the snap from Charlie, faked a handoff to Brian, turned and pitched the ball to Gus, who was running behind both of them. As soon as Gus had the ball in his hands, running left to right, he turned on the jets, turned the corner, put such a smoking-hot move on the Mustangs' left corner that the kid fell down.

Wildcats 13, Mustangs 13.

On the conversion play, Jake carried three guys with him into the end zone. Now it was 14–13, Mustangs. That was the way the game ended.

SEVENTEEN

Teddy was having lunch with Jack and Cassie and Gus on his back patio, just after noon on Sunday.

It had been Teddy's mom who'd suggested they all have lunch together and talk about their community service obligation, how they might be able to work together and somehow save the music department and, ultimately, Mrs. Brandon's job.

"I promise not to wear you all out with this," Alexis Madden said. "Or interfere with the one o'clock football games."

"Not just any one o'clock game," Teddy said. "Giants versus Cowboys."

"I'm aware of that," his mom said. "I'm actually surprised they haven't declared this a national sports holiday."

"I've been meaning to ask you," Cassie said to Teddy. "Now that you're a quarterback, are you giving Eli Manning as much love as Odell Beckham?"

"I have to admit," Teddy said, "that I am feeling the love a little more for Eli these days."

"Can we take the football talk off the table for just a few minutes?" Teddy's mom said.

"They'd rather you took the food," Cassie said.

"If you do, Mrs. Madden, would it be okay if you at least left the chips?" Gus said.

"I sometimes forget what an amusing group this is," Teddy's mom said.

"Think about it, Mom," Teddy said. "Would you want me hanging around with a bunch of humorless losers?"

His mom sighed.

"Could we talk about something that's not at all funny for a few minutes?" she said. "Like Mrs. Brandon losing her job?"

Cassie said, "It's awful. You guys think of whoever your

favorite coaches have ever been, in any spo[...] who Mrs. B is in music. We can't just let them s[...] the door."

Teddy grinned. "Mom just can't let that happen to a [...] mer band member."

"A *what*?" Cassie said.

"Yup," Teddy said. "Mom and Mrs. B used to be in a girl singing group."

"*Get out of here!*" Cassie said. "You were rocking out back in the day, Mrs. Madden?"

"I try to limit my singing around the house," she said. "When the windows are open, it tends to scare the neighbors."

That much Teddy knew about his mom, even if he hadn't known about the Baubles. She was always listening to one of her favorite radio stations, or playing songs from her iPod on the speakers spread throughout the house. And most of the time she *would* be singing along, still knowing all the words to an amazing number of songs.

Jack said, "So what can we do?"

Teddy's mom told them that the town hadn't explained exactly how much money it would take to keep the music program in place at Walton Middle. But she said she had a rough idea of how much it cost, per student, including the price of instruments; and how much money it cost to stage

...ie big holiday show. Mrs. Brandon wasn't going to lose her job at the school. She also taught history. Music, though, was her first love. She had told Cassie once that getting kids to love music made her feel like a writer getting them to want to read.

"Mrs. Brandon likes the night of the show better than she likes Christmas," Cassie said. "We can't let them take that away from her too."

"You mean they might?" Gus said.

"Yeah," Jack said. "I heard my mom talking about it with my dad the other night. She said the town is pretty dug in on this. Without the money we're talking about raising, no holiday show. And my mom thinks that next year, there will be no Mrs. B. She won't stick around if she can't teach music."

Teddy's mom nodded her head. "We've basically got six weeks to come up with the money."

Then she told them that this wasn't just finding a way to accumulate community service hours. This would be a way for them to serve the community at Walton Middle School the way Mrs. Brandon had always served it.

"You four are already a team," Teddy's mom said now. "Probably the coolest team in this town, not just because of how good you all are in sports, but because of the way you look out for each other. I know you all understand the concepts of hard work and *team*work. What I'm asking you to do now is apply all of that to a project like this. Because if we win this one, I promise it will feel as satisfying to you as any championship you've ever won, or ever will win."

"Mom," Teddy said, "do you know how much you just sounded like one of our coaches?"

"Solid pep talk?" she said.

"I was waiting for you make us run some laps," Gus said.

"Listen," she said. "I've never seen anyone as competitive as you all are. I just want you to treat your school's music department like a trophy you're trying to win."

She looked around the table, fixing her eyes on one face after another. "Okay?"

"Okay," they all said.

The table got quiet, until Gus said, "But how?"

"Let's just spitball some ideas," Alexis Madden said. "And there's only one rule of good spitballing: just shout out anything that comes into your head. What you think might be a dumb idea might turn out to be brilliant."

That was what they did. Gus suggested a bake sale. Teddy wondered how much they could make washing cars in the school parking lot every weekend, around their game schedule. Gus said they should raffle off some really good prizes, but he wasn't sure what kind of prizes. Jack said that the trick was coming up with a good charity event without calling it a charity event, so that Mrs. Brandon wouldn't feel as if they were treating her as a charity *case*.

"I've got one," Cassie said.

"Just one?" Teddy said.

"I'll handle trying to raise money on Gofundme.com," she said.

"Go funny?" Gus said.

"Not funny, you idiot. It's this site where you can try to raise money for personal things that really, really matter to you." She looked at Teddy across the table. "Go grab your laptop and I'll show it to you guys."

Teddy jumped right up. He knew the drill. So did Jack and Gus. It hadn't been a request. He came back about two minutes later with his laptop and placed it in front of Cassie. She opened it up and showed them the home page, which had "Crowdfunding for Everyone!" at the top.

They all got behind her and watched as she scrolled down, showing them some of the different reasons for which people were trying to raise money.

"Fix Mrs. Seville's car" was one, with two thousand dollars having been raised so far. There was another one for an ex–newspaper editor with Parkinson's disease, and one for a Massachusetts police officer who'd been injured on the job.

Money had even been raised for a girl's sick puppy.

"But how can we do something like this without Mrs. B thinking we're treating her like some kind of charity case? She is way too cool for that."

"By just telling people that she's *still* a rock star," Cassie said. "By just putting her story out there, about somebody who *does* get kids to love music, and somebody those kids love even more."

"Well," Teddy's mom said, "I know I love this idea. Cassie, you are now our vice president in charge of social media."

Cassie raised an eyebrow. "Only *vice* president?" she said. "What about girl power, Mrs. Madden?"

"You're absolutely right," Teddy's mom said. "You are now president and chief operating officer of social media."

"I'm comfortable with that," Cassie said.

"Now, what about the boys?" Teddy's mom said.

"Maybe your dad could get ESPN to help out?" Gus said.

"No," Teddy said. "Definitely not."

"Why?" Cassie said.

"This isn't his," he said. "This is ours."

But he was looking at his mom as he said it. They both knew what he meant. Teddy wanted it to be hers.

The table got silent again. Teddy checked his phone. There were still ten minutes until the kickoff at MetLife Stadium. It was then that Teddy noticed Jack Callahan smiling, the way he had in football when he was kneeling in the huddle, about to run a play he loved.

"This is about music, right?" he said.

"All about music," Teddy's mom said. "It's about all the music this woman has put into the life of this school for a long time."

"Okay then," Jack said.

"Okay what?" Gus said.

"How about we invent our own version of *The Voice*?" he said. "How about we have the four of us be judges, and have teams, and some elimination rounds, and then we sell tickets to the finals that parents or anybody else who wants to come can buy?"

"Mrs. Brandon can help us with the auditions!" Cassie said.

Without thinking, Teddy said, "Who's gonna be Blake and who's gonna be Adam?"

As soon as the words were out of his mouth he saw Jack and Gus staring at him.

"I thought you said you never watched *The Voice*," Gus said.

"I mean, how would a guy who says he never watches the show know who Blake and Adam are?" Jack said.

Teddy at least had the presence of mind to pull out his phone again and say, "Oh man, it's two minutes until the kick!" Then he nearly ran inside the house.

But before he was through the kitchen door, he heard his mom say, "He's definitely going to want to be Blake."

EIGHTEEN

The next week of practice for Teddy felt like starting school all over again:

Quarterback school.

As much as he thought he knew about the playbook—and he knew more about it than any player on the team except Jack—what he really found out over the next three practices was how much he *didn't* know.

Halfway through Monday night's practice he said to Jack,

"Explain to me again why you've always told me playing this position is such big fun."

"Because it is big fun," Jack said.

Jack had promised Teddy that he was going to make as many practices as he could from now on, his way of trying to help Teddy figure things out on the fly. Teddy told him he didn't have to do that. But he knew this was a way for Jack to contribute to the team.

But they both knew that Jack was only an assistant quarterback coach. Teddy's primary coach was his dad. The other night Teddy had been watching ESPN and heard somebody talking about how fast things changed in sports. Teddy already knew that, because of what had happened during the baseball season. But that was nothing compared to what was happening right now. He'd gone from having no dad in his life to having a full-time dad, at least when he was on the football field.

And practices were different now, especially when they'd scrimmage. If Teddy did something wrong, with a drop or a read or how long he was supposed to hold the ball on a screen pass, Coach Gilbert would blow his whistle, and then Teddy's dad would take the ball and show Teddy exactly what he'd done wrong.

His dad had tried to prepare him before practice.

"There's going to be a lot of repetition," he said. "Reps are how you get better."

"I get it."

"I don't want you to feel like I'm calling you out in front of the team when you do something wrong."

"Got it."

"For real?"

"You don't have to draw me a picture," Teddy said, feeling himself getting irritated even though he knew his dad was just trying to help.

"I just don't want to hurt your feelings."

"You should have started worrying about that a long time ago."

His dad stared at him before he said, "We've got a lot of work to do."

Teddy was sure he wasn't just talking about football.

Starting with Monday's practice, he had a good week, learning a lot about the little things that went into playing the position. The footwork, even on handoffs, began to feel more natural to him, to the point where he didn't have to think about it on every play.

And he kept telling himself not to overthink throwing the ball. It was the point that Jack continued to drive home, that he had to trust his arm.

When they finished with the last practice of the week on Thursday night, Jack said, "You're starting to get something."

"That I wish your shoulder would heal by Saturday?"

"You're doing what my dad says you have to do in any sport," Jack said. "Controlling the process and not freaking out worrying about results."

"Oh good," Teddy said. "One more little factoid I have to remember, until my head explodes."

"You're a fast learner," Jack said.

"Getting into college someday is going to be easier than this," Teddy said.

Jack grinned. "You think you're going to get into college?"

"Watch it," Teddy said. "Or when we start doing *The Voice*, I'll suggest to Cassie that you sing instead of coach."

"I have a plan if that happens," Jack said.

"Really."

"Yeah," he said. "I tell my parents we have to move."

Planning how they wanted to do the singing competition at school had actually been a good thing for Teddy, just because it was the only time in his day when he didn't obsess about football. He could actually feel himself starting to get motivated, same as his friends were, just because the more they talked about it, the more they realized what a cool idea this really was. It was such a good cause for such a good person. Teddy's mom had always told him that the greatest energy source in the world was a random act of kindness.

Sitting on the bench next to Jack now, practice over, shoulder pads off and Teddy feeling the good kind of tired you felt after you'd left everything on the field, Teddy said, "You know that for all the complaining I do to you, I'm excited about starting at QB on Saturday."

"You're ready, dude."

What he wasn't ready for, as he was collecting his equipment, was for his dad to come over and tell them that the night for them to have that burger together had arrived.

"Just checked with your mom," David Madden said. "She's going out with Mrs. Callahan and Mrs. Bennett. I'm dropping you home, waiting while you clean up, and we'll have a boys' night out."

Teddy had learned a lot of good moves this week. He didn't have one to get away from his dad.

"Okay," he said.

NINETEEN

The place was called Back Street.

Teddy had been there a few times with his mom, and everybody in Walton said it had the best burger in town.

They took a booth in the front room, across from the bar. One of the television sets above the bar was showing the Thursday night football game on ESPN. The other two were showing baseball games, one the Yankees and one the Red Sox.

"This was a high school hangout back in the day," David Madden said. "We'd come here after games for burgers and milk shakes. They only turned it into a sports bar after I went off to college. Since then, they haven't even changed the sawdust on the floor, as far as I can tell."

"So this was, like, your place?"

"The best," his dad said. He paused slightly and said, "From the best time in my life."

There it was again. Loving Teddy's mom and having her love him back, that wasn't the best part of his life. Neither was having a son later on. Playing quarterback for Walton High, throwing the ball to his buddy Dick Gilbert, then coming over to Back Street to celebrate another win, that was it for him.

Good times, Teddy thought.

They both ordered cheeseburgers. Teddy didn't eat cheeseburgers as often as he used to, or fries. But he was all-in tonight, mostly because of how hungry he was. At the very least, he told himself, he'd get a good meal out of this.

After the waitress walked away, Teddy fixed his eyes on the TV set showing the football game, Pittsburgh against North Carolina.

"So," his dad said finally, as a way of bringing Teddy back into their booth.

"So."

Teddy looked across the table and saw his dad's smile fixed in place, as usual. By now Teddy knew you could knock that smile off his face. But it wasn't easy.

"How do you think it's going so far?" his dad said.

"You mean in football?"

"We can start there."

"I feel myself *thinking* more like a quarterback," Teddy said. "Using what Jack calls the quarterback brain I didn't know I had. And the big thing is that I realize I don't have to see the whole field at once, even though I want to."

"You can only control what you can control."

Teddy almost said, "Tell me about it." But he didn't. Instead he said, "Maybe it was because Jack made it look so easy. I had no idea there was this much to it, on every single play, even a running play off tackle."

"When people say it's the most important position in sports," his dad said, "they're right. Even at this level."

"No pressure," Teddy said.

"Don't look at it that way," his dad said. "Are you kidding? You gotta treat this like some surprise package that got delivered out of the blue."

"My life is just full of surprises these days," Teddy said.

"Is that a bad thing?"

"I don't know, Dad. You tell me."

Then he turned to look up at the TV set. Pittsburgh's quarterback had just completed a long pass. By the time he got home, he knew, the NFL Thursday night game would be starting, Packers against the Lions. He couldn't wait. He loved watching Aaron Rodgers play, now more than ever. He was the guy in the NFL who made playing quarterback look easy.

"Are we still just talking about football?" David Madden said.

Teddy sighed and turned back to him. "It's *never* just about football," he said, "even when we're on the field. I know you want to help me get better. But you think I can't see you trying to win me over at the same time?"

"And *that*," his dad said, "is a bad thing?"

"It may be working out great for you with my friends." Teddy took in some air, then let it out. "But you didn't leave them."

Now the smile on his dad's face was gone.

Underneath the chatter coming from the people at the bar, he said, "I didn't think of it as leaving you. I left because I couldn't stay."

He waited while the waitress put their plates in front of them. When she was gone, he said, "Does that make any sense at all?"

"It doesn't matter."

"It does to me."

"Whatever I think about it or whatever I say about it, it's not going to change anything."

"It might at least get you to understand where I'm coming from."

"And that's supposed to make everything okay between us?" Teddy said.

"I've told you this before, or at least tried to tell you," David Madden said. "I realize I can't fix the past. It's like trying to go back and do things differently in the game you already lost. I know what I've lost with you. I do. But all I can do is work on right now, the way we're working at football." He leaned forward, his own big hands on the table. "And whether you like it or not, you know we're doing that together."

"I'm happy this has all worked out for you," Teddy said, knowing how sarcastic he sounded, knowing sarcasm still came way too easy to him.

They ate in silence for the next few minutes. Back Street got more crowded. The front room got much louder. Somehow it made the quiet in their booth seem less awkward to Teddy. He wondered if it would ever be as easy for them to have a conversation away from the field as it was on the field.

"I want to help you get better," his dad said finally. "Because I think getting better at quarterback is something that will make you happy."

Teddy had started to take another bite of his burger, but he put it back down.

"*Now*," he said. "Now you want to help me be happy, when it's convenient for you."

His dad started to say something. Teddy stopped him by putting his right hand up. "Please let me finish," he said.

"Okay."

The words came out of him fast and hot. "The way you're always talking about missing high school football? Being that guy? Well, guess what? That's the way I used to miss you, at least until I didn't."

He wondered if his dad might say that he'd missed Teddy, too, because he'd never said that.

He didn't now.

"And I've got to wear that, like guys your age say," his dad said. "I know how much I've screwed up. But as much as you think I've screwed *you* up, I happen to be looking across the table at a pretty great human. So how about we just agree for the time being that what I'm *not* doing is screwing you up as a football player." The smile came back. "At least not yet."

His big right hand came across the table. "Deal?"

Teddy put out his own hand, hesitating just slightly, and shook it.

"Deal," he said.

Teddy wasn't going to admit it in the booth at Back Street, but it happened to be a good deal for him. Maybe even a great deal, because he was getting better as a quarterback, in just one week.

It wasn't the way he'd ever expected, but his dad was finally here for him.

TWENTY

On the way to Holzman Field for the game against Rawson, Alexis Madden said to Teddy, "I'm very proud of you for the way you've accepted your dad."

"Who said anything about accepting him?" Teddy said. "You mean like an invitation? I don't remember being invited to anything. How about we go with tolerating him?"

She smiled. "How about we go with the fact that he doesn't

seem to make your head explode the way he did when he first came back to town?"

"I don't want you to think that just because he's helping me be a better player, that means I think he's a better dad," Teddy said. "They're two different things."

"You never know," she said as they pulled into the parking lot. "Sometimes they can turn out to be the same thing."

"I'm not going to ask you again whose side you're on, because I already know the answer."

"You never know," she said. "Maybe being on your side will turn out to mean I'm on everybody's side."

As he got out of the car, she said, "Oh, and one other thing."

"What?"

"Beat Rawson," she said.

"Now, that," Teddy said, "I can totally accept."

He got out of the car and went to start his first game at quarterback.

Halfway through the second quarter Teddy had figured out exactly how a good quarterback was supposed to do it.

There was just a slight problem:

He wasn't the one doing it.

The Huskies' quarterback, Chris Charles, was a tall, fast

left-hander. Watching him play, you couldn't decide whether he was better running the ball or throwing it. But what wasn't in dispute, at least so far, was that the Wildcats had no idea how to stop him from doing either.

It was 20–7, Huskies. The only reason the Wildcats were on the board at all after falling behind 20–0 was because Gus had made the kind of crazy catch that one of the Seahawks, Jermaine Kearse, had made against the Patriots in the Super Bowl. Teddy had thrown the ball as far as he could on a straight-up fly pattern, Coach Gilbert and Teddy's dad hoping to catch the Huskies napping a little on second-and-one. But the kid covering Gus ran right with him down the sidelines, then timed his jump perfectly as the ball was on its way down. Only he didn't knock the *ball* down in the process, even as Gus stumbled and fell trying to catch the ball himself.

The ball went straight up. When it came down, it hit off Gus's right knee. Then he tipped it with his left hand as he tried to control it. When it finally came to rest, it hit Gus's stomach the way your head hits a pillow, and it was a touchdown for the Wildcats. On the next play Teddy ran a quarterback draw for the conversion.

When Teddy came off the field, he said to his dad, "I know we got lucky and scored. But when I saw how covered Gus was, that was a time when I should have eaten the ball, right?"

"Wrong," David Madden said. "We were down three scores and needed to take a chance. I know rule number one is supposed to be holding the ball when in doubt. But I neglected to tell you rule number two."

"Which is?"

"Sometimes you gotta give one of your guys a chance to make a play."

"And I was that guy!" Gus said, slapping Teddy on the back.

Chris Charles finally made his first mistake with three minutes left in the half. *He* was the one who should have pulled the ball down under pressure. But he hadn't been missing all day, making one kind of hero throw after another even when the Wildcats' defense was all over him. He tried to make another one of those throws now with Max Conte up in his face.

He ran to his left trying to elude Max and threw across his body, hoping to hit his tight end. But the ball floated just enough for Gregg Leonard to pick it off, like it was a ball he was running down in centerfield for their baseball team. Gregg caught it in stride, and by the time one of the Rawson wide receivers caught up with him, he was at the Huskies' forty-yard line.

Jake Mozdean took over from there, starting with a twenty-yard run off tackle. Then, instead of sending Brian in with the next play, Coach left Jake in there, and Teddy knew what that meant:

THE EXTRA YARD

He wanted them to run the same play with Jake again.

They did. Jake found even more daylight this time, Nate Vinton threw a great downfield block, and Jake finally cut the play back to the inside and scored. It was 20–13. On the conversion, Teddy faked a handoff to Jake, straightened up, and hit a wide-open Mike O'Keeffe—and they were down six at the half.

Teddy's dad came over to him after he'd gotten a drink.

"It's a fair fight at quarterback now," he said. "Wasn't at the start. Now it is."

"You're wrong," Teddy said. "The other guy's better."

"No, *you're* wrong," his dad said, some bite in his voice, not smiling now. "There's a lot of things I don't know very much about, and you've already figured out some of them. But about this, I *do* know a lot. And what I know is that you're gonna outplay that guy the second half."

Teddy knew this was no time for a debate. He could see on his dad's face, hear in his voice, that David Madden was in no mood for a debate.

"Okay," he said, before adding, "Coach."

His dad said, "The way he ran it for most of the half? I think you can do the same now that you've made them respect your arm."

Then he was the one giving Teddy a good whack on the back, saying, "Let's do this."

He looked and sounded as excited as Teddy felt about the second half. And he looked happy. One more time Teddy wondered if his dad could ever be quite as happy anywhere else.

Chris Charles wasn't giving up after one bad throw, though. He took the Huskies down the field to start the third quarter, throwing now more than running. It was as if he was trying to keep Coach Williams and the guys on the Wildcats' defense off balance.

Teddy's dad had Teddy stand next to him on the sideline, so he could explain what the Huskies were doing—and trying to do—on offense.

"See," he said, with more than a little admiration in his voice, "it's not just all the game he's got. It's his *feel* for the game. That's a pretty dangerous combination."

"I see what you mean," Teddy said. "He acts surprised when he *doesn't* make a play."

Then they both watched as Chris faked a throw on the run, pulled the ball down, and ran in for the score that made it 26–14 for the Huskies. It stayed that way when Andre Williams elevated at the line of scrimmage and knocked away Chris's pass to his tight end for the conversion.

"Okay," Teddy's dad said, almost as if he were talking to

himself. "We score twice, the defense shuts them down from here, and we win."

"You sound like you're playing Madden," Teddy said. "But this isn't Madden."

"No, kid," he said. "It's way more fun than that."

Maybe it was because his dad's belief was this strong. But in that moment he made Teddy believe too. Maybe, Teddy thought, it was what made him such a good salesman. He made it sound as if Teddy had no choice but to buy in and win the game.

On the next drive Teddy ran the ball three times for big gains, completed passes to Gus, Mike, and Nate. Just like that they were inside the Huskies' ten. On first-and-goal Teddy rolled out to his right and froze the linebacker closest to him, who'd decided that Teddy was going to run the ball again. Only he stopped and hit a wide-open Nate Vinton between the goalposts. Brian McAuley ran behind Charlie Lyons for the conversion. With a minute left in the third quarter, it was Rawson 26, Walton 20.

Coach Gilbert came over and pumped Teddy's hand when he was off the field. "Now it's like you've been under center your whole life," he said.

"Not *even* in my dreams," Teddy said.

Chris Charles got the Huskies driving again, and Teddy was worried they were going to be two touchdowns behind in the fourth quarter, but he threw another interception, off a deflection. The ball ended up in Henry Koepp's hands. Except Teddy gave the ball right back, fumbling after taking a huge blindside hit on a blitz, no chance to fall on the ball after getting blasted sideways.

Rawson ball, midfield, five minutes left. Teddy was slapping the side of his helmet, hard, as he came off the field.

"I should have known they were coming," he said.

His dad laughed. "Seriously?"

"You think this is amusing?"

"Nope," he said. "But Tom Brady would have coughed it up on that hit."

"We gotta get the ball back."

"We will," his dad said. "How many scores did I say we were gonna get after they scored their last touchdown?"

Teddy held up two fingers.

"And how many do we have so far?"

"One."

"It's just simple math," his dad said.

The Huskies made a couple of first downs, but then the Wildcats' defense made its best stand of the whole game. The guys rushed Chris Charles into two incompletions, sacked him once, at the Wildcats' twenty-five. The Huskies decided to go for it even on fourth-and-long, knowing that a first down for them might be the same as ending the game. They tried a gadget play, a halfback pass, but before the kid could get the ball off, Max Conte came flying in from middle linebacker and leveled him.

Two minutes and twenty seconds left. Wildcats ball. Sixty-nine yards away. Teddy started to run back on the field but felt Coach Gilbert's hand on his shoulder. "You got this?"

"I got this," Teddy said.

His dad said, "Is there any play you don't think you can run?"

Teddy turned and looked at him. Now the bite was in his voice. "I *said* I got this."

"Music to my ears," his dad said.

Jack was there too. "Hey," he said.

"What is this, a quiz?" Teddy said.

"Simple question," Jack said. "Would you have signed up for this when we were down 20–zip?"

"Totally."

"Good answer."

Teddy hit Nate for six yards on first down, missed Gus—badly—on second. The Huskies were looking for a pass on third-and-four, but Teddy gave it to Jake, who wouldn't let them tackle him until he had the first down. Teddy hit Mike O'Keeffe, and they were in Huskies' territory. They were moving. But so was the clock.

A little over a minute left. Two time-outs in Coach Gilbert's pocket. But Teddy wasn't looking at him—or Jack—when he looked over to the sideline. Almost despite himself, he was looking at his dad. For the last time today, he was trying to make David Madden's belief his own. He'd try to figure out later what it meant. Just not right now at Holzman Field.

He hit Gus in traffic in the middle of the field, no fear in the throw, none. He looked over to the sideline, seeing if Coach wanted to use one of his time-outs, fifty seconds left. All Coach did was nod and keep Brian McAuley next to him.

The nod meant throw the same pass to Gus again.

The Huskies weren't expecting that, so Gus was more open this time. A lot more open. Now they were at the twenty. Clock running. There were no time-outs for first downs in their league. The clock kept running.

Finally Coach called one.

Teddy sprinted over to the sideline. When he got there, Jack handed him his water bottle. Teddy tipped his helmet back on his head and took a long swallow.

"We could run it and run some clock," Coach Gilbert said.

"Doesn't matter," Teddy's dad said. "They're done whenever we score."

When. Not if.

"Then why wait?" Coach Gilbert said. "We never did in the old days."

"How about the last play we ran for a touchdown, to Nate?"

It was like they were having a private conversation, and Teddy was just there eavesdropping.

"Love it," Coach Gilbert said.

He gave Teddy a small shove back toward the field. "Go win the game," he said.

Teddy rolled to his right, pulled up, threw a slightly longer pass to Nate this time. He was open again, right there between the posts. And they won the game.

"Told you," Teddy's dad said to him when he got back to the sideline. "Simple math."

Then, before Teddy could do anything about it, his dad hugged him.

TWENTY-ONE

On days when there was no football practice—or even when there was a late practice—Teddy and his friends threw themselves into their production of *The Voice*.

By now Mrs. Brandon was helping them. Her reasoning, as she explained, was simple: she wasn't doing it for herself, she was doing it for the school, because she believed no school should be without music.

They were meeting in Mrs. Brandon's office today, and there

was even more excitement than usual in the room, because they had been given a date for the show. The next step was to decide how much to charge adults, how much to charge students, and what the best way was to start selling tickets in advance.

Before long, though, Teddy and Jack and Gus were going at one another about being coaches in the competition, and how each of them was sure his team was going to win.

Cassie looked at Mrs. Brandon and sadly shook her head. "Boys," she said, as if that explained everything in the universe. "All they care about is keeping score."

"I am so winning this," Jack said, "even with one hand tied behind my back."

"You do remember your sling came off a week ago, right?" Teddy said.

"Figure of speech, dude. Figure of speech."

They were going to start auditions next week. The finals would be three weeks later, on a Thursday night. So far Cassie had gotten more than two thousand dollars in donations on the Internet. She vowed that they hadn't seen anything yet—she was just getting started.

The best part of it was that Mrs. Brandon was now as excited about the project as they were. Just not as excited as Teddy's mom, who was as full of ideas as ever, about how she thought the stage should look on the big night, about how there should be a student master of ceremonies; even about hiring a local band to back up the singers.

Then they were all talking about ticket prices, because the show needed to be the biggest part of the fund-raising if they wanted to have any chance of saving Mrs. Brandon's department.

"It's tricky," Mrs. Brandon said. "We want to bring in as much money as possible. But at the same time we don't want to scare people off."

"People in town will support a good cause," Teddy's mom said, "even if some of the jerks in city government won't."

Teddy turned and high-fived Gus. "Jerks," he said. "Listen to the chirp from Mom."

"Are you making fun of your mother?" Mrs. Brandon said.

"Just making an observation," Teddy said.

"In the end," his mom said, "we are going to show those people how wrong they were."

"Light 'em up, Mrs. Madden!" Gus said.

Then she was the one high-fiving Gus. "That's what I'm talking about," she said.

"Mrs. M," Cassie said, "this is the most fired up I've ever seen you about anything."

"You think only the men in my family are competitive?" she said. "Well, you haven't seen anything yet."

Then she told everybody to follow her out of the office, it was never too early to start thinking about set design.

"*Set design?*" Teddy said.

He looked at his friends. "We've created a monster."

"Is there a problem?" his mom said.

"Absolutely not, Coach Madden," Teddy said.

His mom punched him in the arm the way Cassie did sometimes.

It was the Thursday night practice before their next game, against the Clements Spartans, on the road. Gus's dad had dropped them off way early, because this was one of the nights of the week when he worked the four-to-midnight shift at the car service for which he'd been working since he'd settled his family in Walton. He had started his life in America in New York City after moving there with his own parents from the Dominican Republic. Gus had even been born in New York. But he had no memories of it, having grown up in Walton from the time he was two.

Tonight Mr. Morales had a late-night pickup and then a long drive home from the airport. But he didn't complain. He never complained about anything. Gus never complained about much either. The only time Teddy could remember Gus getting really mad, at anybody, was after Jack had briefly quit their Little League team last spring. Gus didn't understand why Jack had done it. Jack originally didn't tell Gus or anybody else that he blamed himself for his brother's accident.

Once Gus—along with Teddy and Cassie—found out, he and Jack went back to being as close as they'd ever been. And Gus went back to being the happiest kid Teddy knew, except when they lost a game.

Today he told Teddy he'd run pass patterns until the other kids arrived. Teddy said he didn't want Gus to tire himself out before practice began. Gus said that if he didn't want to run the patterns, he wouldn't have said anything.

So that's what they did for more than half an hour, and Teddy could see their timing getting better and better. He knew he'd never have the timing with Gus that Jack had before he got hurt. Jack had been the quarterback and Gus the star wide receiver on every team the two of them had ever played on.

But they were getting there.

Teddy was learning to trust that Gus would be exactly where he was supposed to be the way Teddy trusted his throwing arm. More and more, especially on the cuts that required almost perfect timing, Teddy would release the ball before Gus even turned to look for it.

When they stopped, Gus said to him, "So how we looking?"

"You tell me," Teddy said as the two of them stretched out in the grass. "You're the guy who makes me look like I know a lot more about what I'm doing than I really do."

"Are you kidding?" Gus said. "You get better with every practice."

He stuck his elbow in the grass and put his head in his hand. "But I wasn't asking about football so much."

Teddy groaned. "You too, dude? Now you want to have the father-son talk with me?"

Gus barked out a laugh. "Not *that* talk!" he said.

"Can't we please talk about something else?"

"Nope."

"Well, if you're asking me how things are between my dad and me, they're pretty okay lately."

"Just okay?"

"Yeah," Teddy said. "*Just* okay. Unless I'm supposed to just forget that he hasn't been around for the last eight years."

"*That* doesn't sound okay," Gus said. "That sounds like you're still mad."

"But not mad at you."

"I know," Gus said, grinning at him. "It's practically impossible to get mad at me."

"Try me, if you don't change the subject."

Teddy was sitting cross-legged. He leaned over and checked his phone. It was still a half hour, at least, before they'd start seeing any of their teammates. But he was good with that. It was easy being with Gus, unless you wanted him to change the subject.

"You want my opinion?" Gus said.

"So I guess we're not changing the subject."

Gus rolled over and sat up, so he was looking directly at Teddy. "I think you need to start trusting him. Your dad."

"Not there yet," Teddy said. "Not even close. Not even sure I'll ever get there."

"Why?"

"*Why?*" Teddy said. "Because he hasn't earned it, that's why."

"How does he do that?"

"By not leaving again."

Gus just stared at him.

"Wait a second," he said. "He can't leave. He just moved back."

"He left before."

"But that was, well, that *was* before," Gus said. "And when he did leave, he stayed in one place all that time."

"Maybe he won't like ESPN and want to go back," Teddy said. "Or go someplace else."

"But why are you expecting something bad to happen?" Gus said. "You can't go through your life expecting bad stuff to happen. That's no way to be."

"You don't know anything about bad stuff," Teddy said. "Your life has always been good. It's why you're *you*."

They were quiet again. Teddy knew the field would get loud as soon as their teammates started piling out of their parents' cars. Just not yet.

"I get why you started off being mad at him," Gus said, "especially when he just sort of walked in and became part of our team."

"You *think*?"

"But now you both got past that and things are good," Gus said. "Or at least a lot better."

"I'm happy that you're happy," Teddy said.

"Go ahead and be sarcastic," Gus said. "But I'm right about this. You need to trust your dad."

"I do," Teddy said. "As long as we're on the field."

"*Dude,*" Gus said, stepping on the word. "You gotta listen to me. You don't see the look on his face when you make a good throw to somebody besides me. Or you make a good run. The guy looks like he's over the moon."

"I understand he wants me to do well."

"*Dude!*" Gus said again. "Do you trust me?"

"You know I do."

"Then trust me that you gotta start trusting him."

After practice ended, Teddy's dad asked if he wanted to do a little extra work. Teddy said sure. Then he asked Gus the same thing, and Teddy knew what the answer was going to be. Gus would stay until it was dark if you asked him to, and even after that.

David Madden wanted Teddy to work on what he called his "arm slot." He was constantly telling Teddy that if you were serious about being a good quarterback, you could never get loose with your mechanics, and he'd seen Teddy dropping his arm down tonight without even knowing he was doing it.

"I love Tony Romo's heart," Teddy's dad said. "And the kid from Detroit, Matthew Stafford, he's got a world of talent the way Romo does. But the two of them have awful mechanics, to the point where I don't even want to watch sometimes."

"Then watching me must be like watching a horror movie," Teddy said.

"Quite the contrary," his dad said, shaking his head. "You usually have a beautiful throwing motion." He winked at Teddy and said, "Sometimes I feel like I'm watching myself when I was your age. You know, back when it was all still ahead of me."

He had that faraway look on his face he'd get sometimes when he'd talk about his playing days.

"You still miss it, Mr. Madden?" Gus said.

"Only every day."

"Even now?"

"Let me tell you both something about sports," David Madden said. "You never know how good you have it until you don't have it."

He put his big smile back on then and said, "But you guys, you've both got it going on. Now let's run some of our stuff and fix what I saw from my kid tonight."

They stayed out there until it did start to get dark. When they finished, Teddy's dad said, "Okay, *now* we're ready for Saturday."

"Best day of the week," Teddy said.

"You better be ready," his dad said. "Because we're going to open this offense up. Spring training is over. Time for you to cut it loose."

They beat Clements. Teddy did get to throw more, even after a couple of early interceptions, coming back to throw two touchdown passes to Gus and one to Jake. The final score was 19–7. They were 4–0.

They won again the next Saturday, in a heavy rain, against Ridgeway. It was a mess of a day and a mess of a game. But somehow the Wildcats made it down the field in the fourth quarter, and Teddy got enough of a grip on a wet ball to throw a touchdown pass to Mike O'Keeffe with two minutes left.

As soon as Mike caught the ball, Teddy turned around

quickly enough to see the look on his dad's face that Gus had talked about. His dad was soaking wet, the way everybody else was, his old Walton High cap pulled down tight over his eyes.

It wasn't just that he looked happy. It was more than that. He looked young.

It was as if for one more afternoon he'd gotten back everything that he'd lost when he had it better than he knew, even if somebody else was throwing the game-winning passes now.

TWENTY-TWO

It was halftime of the Giants–Redskins game on Sunday, Eli Manning already having thrown three touchdown passes, two to Odell Beckham Jr. Normally that would have been a cause for great excitement. Just not today.

Today, Teddy and Jack and Gus and Cassie were watching in Jack's basement, all of them—even Cassie—still trying to process what the Wildcats players had learned the day before: that the finals for All-American Football, the league's Super

Bowl, would be played at MetLife Stadium in New Jersey. On the same field where Eli and Beckham were playing right now. They first had to win their league title, and then win their county. But if they did, they were going to MetLife to play for the title the first Saturday after Thanksgiving.

"I still can't believe it," Gus said.

"Same," Teddy said. "We nearly closed the deal in the Little League World Series. Maybe we can do it now in football."

"In *that* stadium," Gus said, pointing at the television screen.

"On *that* field," Teddy said.

"Long way to go, though," Jack said.

Gus said, "We could be ahead by two touchdowns in the last minute of the championship game and you'd still be telling us not to get ahead of ourselves."

"Let's just get there first," Jack said.

On the halftime show, the guys seated at the desk were laughing their heads off.

"When *I'm* on television," Cassie said, "you're not going to see me acting as if everything is that hilarious." She turned to Teddy. "By the way, are you coming when we go up to ESPN with your dad?"

Teddy had the remote in his hand. He muted all the laughter coming from the set.

"*What* trip to ESPN?"

"He just mentioned it after the game yesterday when you'd gone over to be with your mom," she said. "He said he was going to ask you if you wanted to do it next Sunday, because the Giants play at night."

"Well, he didn't mention it to me."

"He probably just forgot before he left," Gus said. "No biggie."

"It is to me," Teddy said. "He should have asked me before he asked you guys." He turned his attention to Cassie. "And how come you didn't mention it?"

"I just did."

"I mean last night."

"I didn't talk to you last night!" Cassie said.

"You're the one who wants to be the television star," Teddy said. "Maybe my dad should just take you."

"Teddy Madden, stop this right now," she said.

She didn't make any attempt to hide the exasperation in her voice, or maybe just the anger. Just like that, she was in what Gus liked to call her "extra-chafe" mode.

"Stop what?" Teddy said, not backing down. "He makes a plan with my friends before he checks it out with me? Not cool."

Cassie stood up. "You're the one being not cool," she said. "And I would like to talk to you outside."

"The second half is about to start," Teddy said. "And why

can't Jack and Gus hear what you have to say?"

"Because right now this is between you and me," she said. "They can pause the game till we get back."

"Don't make this a thing, Cass," he said.

"The thing will be me going home if you don't come outside with me."

She walked up the stairs. Teddy made a helpless gesture to Jack and Gus but followed her. As usual when she *was* in her extra-chafe mode, he felt like he was on his way to the principal's office.

As much as the four of them did think of themselves as a team, there was no question who the captain was.

When they were out in the front yard, Teddy said, "What did I say that was so wrong?"

"What's wrong," she said, "is you acting as if you have the right to hand out grades to your father every single day!"

She was pacing in front of him, even hotter now than she had been inside. "You need to figure out that it doesn't work that way, whether your parents are divorced or not!"

"You don't know anything about divorced parents," Teddy said in a quiet voice.

"It's not about that, and you know it," Cassie said. "It's only about one parent. Your dad. Who as far as I can tell is working his *butt* off to make things right between the two of you. Including this trip to ESPN."

"Gus told me I need to trust him more," Teddy said. "And I'm trying. But then something like this happens."

"You've got to stop jumping on every little thing!" Cassie said. She was shouting at him now. "You act like him making this invitation, especially to me because he knows I'm interested in television, is something bad. Only it's not bad. The way him coming back hasn't turned out to be bad, has it?"

He had no choice but to give her an honest answer. "No."

"Not only is it not bad," she said, "it's actually turned out good."

"So far," Teddy said. "So far, so good."

"Just admit that he's not only making you a better football player," she said, "he's starting to give you what you always wanted, even if you said you didn't: a real dad."

"You think we're one big happy family, Cass? Come on, you know better than that."

"You've finally got two parents in your life, whether they're married to each other or not."

Teddy looked at her. She had her hands on her hips and was still breathing hard. Her face was still a little red. But she had calmed down.

He smiled.

"You're right," he said.

She smiled back.

"I'm sorry," she said, "I didn't quite catch that."

"Do I need to post it on Facebook?" Teddy said.

"That won't be necessary," Cassie said. "Just hearing it is enough."

"It must be so difficult for you," Teddy said, still smiling, "being the bigger person all the time."

"I manage," she said.

Behind them, Gus opened the door and poked his head out.

"Beckham just scored again," he said.

"I thought you were going to pause the game!" Teddy said.

"We're weak," Gus said.

Teddy and Cassie followed him back downstairs. Teddy's dad called after dinner and asked him about ESPN, apologizing for not mentioning it before Teddy left the field. Teddy told him no worries, it was a cool idea and he couldn't wait. His dad said he would go ahead and set it up.

"But we only go if we beat Norris on Saturday, okay?" Teddy said.

Norris was 5–0, the same as the Wildcats. It would be the biggest game they'd played yet.

"Deal," his dad said. "Now go study your new plays so you'll be ready to run them at practice."

"Yes, Coach."

The other guys were starting to call him Coach. There was

no reason for Teddy not to do the same. Coach Gilbert seemed more and more comfortable turning over the play calling to his old quarterback during games and adding things to the Wildcats' offense on the fly. So every few days he'd give the guys a play or two that hadn't been in their playbooks when the season started.

While Teddy had been watching the Giants play this afternoon, his dad had stopped by with more new pages to stick in the back of Teddy's blue binder. It was getting thicker all the time. Sometimes Teddy imagined those pages to be like another new chapter in the story they were writing together.

Like with any really good story, Teddy couldn't wait to find out how this one came out.

TWENTY-THREE

The Norris game was at home, and the bleachers on both sides of Holzman Field were completely full a half hour before the game started. All week long Walton kids and Norris kids had been going back and forth about the game on Facebook—all of it in good fun—as a way of hyping up the battle of the league's two unbeatens.

It was 14–13, Walton, at halftime, and so far the game had lived up to all the hype. Teddy had come out on fire, not even throwing his first incompletion until the Wildcats' second drive. By the time that drive ended, he had thrown for one touchdown and run for another, and the Wildcats were ahead 14–0.

It turned out, though, that the Norris Panthers had a pretty fancy quarterback of their own named Scotty Hanley. He looked too small to play the position as well as he did, or have the kind of arm that he did. But once his team got behind, he began to show you how much game he had. On the Wildcats' sideline, Jack Callahan called him a "wizard."

"Great," Teddy said. "So you're telling me we're up against Harry Potter?"

As small as Scotty Hanley was—and he was the smallest player on either team—he wasn't just playing big. He was playing huge, throwing the ball short and long, hiding it on fakes, running like a streak of light when he got into the open field.

"Pay attention to this guy," Teddy's dad said on the sideline. "You can learn from him."

"I thought I was trying to *beat* him," Teddy said.

"You will," his dad said. "Doesn't mean you can't pick up a few pointers along the way. He's having so much fun it's like he's playing touch football in the street with his buddies."

"And watching him do it is supposed to be fun for me?"

"It's your best against his best today," David Madden said. "What can be better than that?"

Scotty Hanley got the ball first in the second half, and the whole drive was like a clinic on how to play quarterback when you were twelve years old. Or maybe at any age.

A few plays into the drive Scotty sold a fake to his halfback so well, and got to the outside so fast on a bootleg, Teddy thought he was going to run sixty yards for a score. But as fast as he was, Gregg Leonard was faster, and brought him down from behind at the Wildcats' fifteen. Two short passes later Scotty got away from what looked like a sure sack, scrambled to his left, then threw back across his body to his tight end. The touchdown made it 19–14, Norris. Scotty then surprised everybody by running a simple quarterback sneak for the conversion, and it was 20–14.

"He's not going to give this to us," Teddy said, snapping his chin strap, ready to get after it.

"Who wants him to?"

"You're right," Teddy said. "We're just gonna take it."

"Ball fake on first down to Jake, then throw it as far as you can to Gus."

"Love it," Teddy said.

"Let's show the little wizard who's got more tricks up his sleeve," his dad said.

Teddy sold the ball fake to Jake the way Scotty Hanley had been selling fakes like that all game long. Then he stepped back as Gus blew past the cornerback covering him, and he let the ball go. By the time Gus caught it, he was ten yards clear of the cornerback, who would have needed a fast car to catch him. It was 20–20. Jake tripped over Charlie Lyons's foot as he tried to break through the line on the conversion.

So the game between the two unbeaten teams in the league stayed tied, all the way until there were five minutes left in the fourth quarter and Teddy got hurt.

TWENTY-FOUR

It wasn't even that bad a hit.

Teddy tried to hold the ball a second too long even though he could feel the rush coming from his left. When he finally did release the ball, he overthrew Nate, and badly, on the right sideline.

As soon as he did, he got launched sideways, and when he landed, it was on his right shoulder. He felt as if he'd been dropped out of his bedroom window, and he stayed down, the pain shooting through him.

When he finally rolled over, he saw his dad and Coach Gilbert and Dr. McAuley staring down at him.

"Where's it hurt?" his dad said.

"Behind the shoulder, pretty much," Teddy said. "But I'm fine." He sat up.

"How about we let Doc tell you whether you're fine or not?" his dad said.

"We're going to get you over to the sideline so I can take a closer look," Dr. McAuley said. "But before we do, I want you, as gently as possible, to make a big circle with your right arm. And if the pain is too bad, I want you to stop."

Teddy tried, and couldn't help himself from making a face as he followed through. His dad noticed. They probably all did.

"You're coming out," his dad said, as if he were acting as the head coach in that moment.

"No!" Teddy said. "I got dinged is all. It happens to guys on every play in football. Coach Gilbert, you tell us that all the time."

Coach nodded. "Let's just get you over to the sideline so Doc can do what he wants and check the damage."

"There is no damage!" Teddy said. "It was just a hard hit. Please don't make me come out."

"Just for now," Coach Gilbert said. "If there is something wrong, I don't want to make it worse."

"You mean like I did," David Madden said to him.

They all helped Teddy to his feet, even though he told them he didn't need help, and walked him off the field. Teddy was aware of the cheers coming from the Walton side of Holzman Field. He watched from the sideline as Jake, who'd gone in for him at quarterback, tried to get the first down on a quarterback sweep. But Norris's middle linebacker read the play beautifully and dropped Jake for a five-yard loss. Gregg Leonard, the Wildcats' punter, got off a great kick, one that went over the head of the Norris kid trying to return it and finally came to rest at the Norris ten yard line.

Four minutes and one second left. Game still tied at 20-all.

Dr. McAuley had Teddy sit on the bench and put him through a bunch of range-of-motion exercises. Gus stood right there and watched. So did Jack, his eyes big, probably wondering if the same thing that had happened to his shoulder—and his season—had just happened to Teddy.

But it hadn't.

When Doc was finished, he turned to Coach Gilbert and Teddy's dad and said, "I think the boy made an excellent diagnosis. I think it's just a stinger."

"He should get an X-ray, just to be on the safe side," Teddy's dad said.

"*You're not a doctor!*" Teddy said.

"I'm your dad," he said. "And I used to be a quarterback, until I thought I was good to go after a hit like that. It wasn't a sack with me. I got downfield ahead of a ballcarrier and tried to throw a hero block. As soon as I did, I knew something was wrong. But it was a close game like this one, and I told myself I could play through it. And you know what happened? Before long I was going, going, *gone*."

"You got hurt throwing a block?" Teddy said. "You never told me that."

"Even though I was a quarterback, I wanted everybody to know I was a *player*. So I tried to play through an injury, and before long my career was over. I don't want that to happen to you."

"But there's a difference between getting hurt and being injured, right, Doc?" Teddy said.

"I've never heard it put exactly that way," Dr. McAuley said. "But yes, there is a difference."

"If it was Brian, would you let him keep playing?"

"I would."

Teddy's dad, his voice loud, said, "Well, this is about my son, not yours."

"But it's still my team," Coach Gilbert said. "And on my team, we go by what the doctor says. And if the doctor says Teddy can play, he can play."

That didn't just shut up Teddy's dad. It shut up everybody until Teddy said to Coach, "Can I talk to my dad for a minute?"

The other adults walked away. So did Jack and Gus. Now it was just Teddy and his dad, sitting next to each other on the bench.

On the field Scotty Hanley had just been chased out of the pocket and had thrown wildly on third-and-long, which meant that the Wildcats were about to get the ball back.

"Before you say anything, hear me out," Teddy's dad said.

"Talk fast," Teddy said, "because I'm going back in."

"It's your *arm*," his dad said.

"You're right, Dad," he said. "It is my arm."

He got up and walked over to Coach Gilbert as Jake was calling for a fair catch on the Panthers' punt, and said, "I really am good to go."

Coach turned and shot a quick look at Teddy's dad. Teddy turned and saw his dad hesitate, then nod.

"You get hit like that again, you're coming right back here," Coach said.

Teddy grinned. "The only place I'm going is *there*." He

pointed toward the Panthers' end zone. Now Coach grinned.

"You know," he said, "you might be more like your old man than you think."

They started at the Panthers' thirty-nine yard line. When Teddy got to the huddle, Gus said, "Can you throw if you have to?"

Teddy said, "Can you catch if you have to?"

He handed the ball to Jake on first down. Jake got four yards, off right tackle. Then Brian got two more on second down, running to his left. While Teddy waited for Nate to come in with the next play, he checked the clock. Two minutes and ten seconds left. If they could get a score in that time, they would be the only undefeated team in the league.

He rotated his shoulder without making a big show of doing it. It still hurt. He wondered if they were going to let him throw on third-and-four. Or if they were going to run it twice if they had to.

Jake said, "Tight end curl."

Teddy nodded. It was a ten-yard pattern. Coach Gilbert and his dad were going to find out right here if he could make a good throw that far.

He went with a quick count, faked a handoff to Jake, set himself in the pocket, didn't even wait for Mike O'Keeffe to turn around before he brought his arm forward. He felt a twinge as he did. But he didn't baby the throw. It was a spiral, right on Mike O'Keeffe's number 88. Mike secured the ball with both arms right before he got hit by both a safety and a linebacker. First down, Panthers' twenty-four. Under two minutes.

When Mike got back to the huddle, he nodded at Teddy and said, "Boy can play hurt."

"Boy can play, period," Gus said.

"Let's close this deal," Teddy said.

But he got buried on the next play, what was supposed to be a pass to Gus. The Panthers came with an all-out blitz, including one of their safeties, right up the middle. Teddy had no time to even throw the ball away. Or get away from the rush. He managed to cover up, but the kid coming from his right landed on his throwing shoulder.

Teddy wasn't sure, but he thought the kid gave him a little shove as he started to get up. When he did, it was Teddy who was popping up off the ground and rolling the kid, number 58, off him.

"Hey," the kid said.

"Hey what?" Teddy said, taking a step forward. "I'm not your mattress."

Number 58 took a step toward him now. But Gus was there to walk Teddy back to the huddle.

"Feeling something on the shoulder?" Gus said.

"Just feeling it," Teddy said, still eyeballing number 58.

"Like you said," Gus said. "Let's close this deal."

"You're right," Teddy said. "Let's not waste any more time."

But he felt himself smiling. Sometimes getting knocked down just made it feel all that much better when you got up. He looked over at the sidelines. Coach Gilbert and his dad were still about five yards out on the field, as if wondering how he was after taking a shot like that.

Teddy just waved them off.

Forty-five seconds left. Second-and-sixteen. Teddy faked to Jake again and threw a dart to Gus on the left sideline for ten yards. Third-and-six. The clock stopped.

Brian brought in the play: quarterback option roll. It was one of the new plays his dad had put in for this game. Teddy had the option of making a quick slant throw to Gus or pulling the ball down and running for the chains himself.

As they broke the huddle, Teddy said, "Like I asked you before: Can you catch?"

"Try me."

But the Panthers' middle linebacker, who'd made smart decisions the whole game, made another one now. He read the play perfectly, jumping Gus's route as he came across the field from the left slot, almost daring Teddy to throw into his area.

He almost did. His arm was already coming forward when

he spied the middle linebacker. But his big right hand saved him again and turned what was going to be a throw into a world-class pump fake, the kind Scotty Hanley had been making for his team all day.

Teddy decided to run for it, putting a good move on the Panthers' outside linebacker and getting a step on him to the outside, realizing he didn't just have a chance for a first down now, he had a chance to score.

He was at the five yard line by then and could see the middle linebacker who'd taken the pass to Gus away from him coming hard from his left, trying to cut him off.

Teddy didn't hesitate. He took one more long stride and then dove for the orange pylon, flying through the air with the ball in both hands, trying to make the same kind of play Jack had been trying to make when he wrecked his own right shoulder.

Out of the corner of his eye he saw the middle linebacker launch himself at the same time.

No fear from him, no fear from Teddy Madden. He was trying to win the game right here, and the other kid was doing anything he could to stop him from doing that, even if it meant a midair collision.

But this time the other kid missed. He landed behind Teddy. Teddy landed a couple of yards past the pylon, in the end zone and inbounds.

He didn't land on his shoulder this time. Just the football. It knocked all the wind out of him. He didn't care, because he knew in that moment he'd basically knocked the Norris Panthers right into second place.

Yeah, Teddy thought.

Yeah, he could play hurt even if he couldn't catch his breath right now.

When he got to the sideline after Brian ran in for the conversion, his dad came up to him and started to slap him on the shoulder, but he stopped himself just in time.

"That shoulder must be made out of rock," his dad said.

"Nah," Teddy said. "Just my head."

"Now that," Coach Gilbert said, "*does* run in the family."

TWENTY-FIVE

The trip to ESPN on Sunday afternoon turned out to be a lot of fun.

They walked around what was known as the "campus" and really looked like one. They toured the sets where the network had done their NFL shows in the morning and would do them again later at night. They also saw the sets for the *Baseball Tonight* show, and *SportsCenter,* and where they did the *Mike & Mike* show during the week.

Teddy's dad showed them a couple of control rooms for *SportsCenter*, where he said the producers and directors and the technical people sat. There was another huge room, what looked to Teddy to be the size of a football field, where researchers, some of them not looking all that much older than Teddy and his friends, sat staring at computer terminals.

"What are they all doing, looking up the same stuff?" Gus said.

"No," Teddy's dad said. "They're trying to find stuff that nobody else has, before somebody else finds it first."

From there they walked past a cafeteria and down a long corridor to the studios for ESPN Radio. Teddy's dad pointed out where the host was sitting on one side of the glass, and where the producers sat on the other.

Teddy could see his dad thoroughly enjoying himself, acting as their tour guide and an expert on everything they were seeing. But Cassie was enjoying this tour the most, asking the most questions.

At one point Teddy whispered to her, "It's like you're trying to memorize this place."

"I want to know my way around when I come back someday for work," she said.

"So you're going to be the second coming of Hannah Storm?"

"No," she said. "Just the first Cassie Bennett."

"Hey," Teddy's dad said, "you might be working for me when you do."

"You looking to be a boss, Dad?" Teddy said.

"How great would that be?" his dad said. "Someday I'm gonna be the one calling the plays around here."

Teddy's dad led them back outside, to the middle of the campus, where there were signs telling them how many miles away places like Wimbledon were. Cassie poked Teddy with an elbow and said, "Thank your dad for doing this."

"Can't I wait until we're through?"

"No," she said. "Thank him now and then thank him again later, so he'll know you really mean it. This has been, like, the best field trip ever."

"Why can't you tell him that?"

She sighed and shook her head. "You can be so thick sometimes," she said. "You do get that it will mean more coming from you, right?"

"But won't it technically be coming from you, since you're making me say it?"

She stopped him by putting a hand on his shoulder. "The next elbow will hurt."

They picked up the pace and caught up with the others. When they did, Teddy said, "Dad, thank you *so* much." He glanced at Cassie and said, "This has been the best field trip *ever.*"

"You're welcome, kid," his dad said. He looked right at Teddy then as he said, "Sometimes you just gotta take a quick step back and appreciate things that are right in front of you."

He was still looking at Teddy when he said in a soft voice, "I'm actually the one who should be thanking all of you."

When they started walking again, Cassie stuck another elbow in Teddy's ribs. It *did* hurt, as promised.

"You're welcome," she said.

TWENTY-SIX

The semifinals for the Walton Middle School version of *The Voice* were set for Thursday, at a last-period assembly.

They'd set up the competition a lot differently from the way they did the real *Voice* on television. But with two shows to go, Teddy and Jack and Gus and Cassie each had one singer still competing for the trophy the school was going to provide, along with a one-hundred-dollar cash prize. Two singers would be eliminated at the assembly.

In a week they'd put on their big show, the biggest in the history of the school, and declare a winner. But for now, there was constant chatter on social media, with kids in the school picking sides. As far as Teddy could tell, the majority of kids in the school thought Katie Cummings, the last singer for Team Cassie, was the favorite to walk away with the trophy and the cash.

Teddy's singer was Gregg Leonard, from the Wildcats. Gregg had shocked everybody on their team by not only trying out, but also by having a great singing voice. Jack had Vi Odierno, whose mother had been a professional singer and who had a pretty great voice of her own. Gus had his twin sister Angela. None of them were conceding anything to Coach Cassie and Katie. They were all competing to the end. The fact that this was for such a good cause just made the whole thing feel more intense, especially as they got closer to the finals.

Tonight, at Teddy's house, they were having their last meeting before the assembly. His mom was there, and Mrs. Brandon, and the four coaches. They'd cleared away the pizza boxes from the dining room table and were going over last-minute details, wondering if there was anything they had missed.

"Mom," Teddy said, "there have been invasions we studied in history that weren't as well planned as this."

"God is in the details," she said.

Teddy pointed at Cassie and said, "Write that down!"

His mom narrowed her eyes. "I know you're funny, young man. Just not as funny as you think you are."

"I tell him that all the time," Cassie said.

"Maybe you're the one not as funny as you think you are," Gus said.

"Be quiet," Cassie said to him. "Or I'll tell everybody you're rooting harder for Katie than for your own sister."

Gus said, "I'm not saying another word the rest of the night."

Teddy's mom had a sheet of paper in front of her that broke down how much money they'd raised so far from ticket sales, how much from the Internet, and how much from sponsorships they'd been able to sell to some local businesses. She took off her reading glasses, stuck them on top of her head, and sighed loudly.

"We're still not there," she said.

"But the show's going to be great, Mrs. M," Jack said. "I swear, kids are talking more about *The Voice* than they are about the Wildcats going for the championship."

"This isn't about what's good, or right," Mrs. Brandon said. "Teddy's mom is talking about what's real. And what's real here is the bottom line."

"You kids are always telling me there's a reason why they keep score in sports, right?" Teddy's mom said. "All I'm doing is looking at the scoreboard. And our team is still losing."

"What if we do lose?" Cassie said. "Do we just give the money we've raised to the school, and it's over for the music department and Mrs. Brandon?"

Teddy's mom surprised them all by slapping the table. "We are not losing!" she said. "You guys are going for your Super Bowl? Well, this is mine."

When everybody had left, Teddy and his mom sat in the living room, music playing softly in the background. With Teddy's football season and *The Voice* planning, there hadn't been much quiet time like this for the two of them, at least not lately.

"You've been on some roll," his mom said.

"You mean with the Wildcats?"

"I mean with the Wildcats and with your dad."

"I guess."

"You *guess*?" she said. "Please remember that when he first came back to town, you thought it was going to be a total disaster."

"Like one of those disaster movies."

"Now you haven't lost," she said. "And it looks to me as if you've gained a dad."

"A football dad." He grinned. "Let's see how he does when he's out of season."

"I know you're joking," she said. "But the past few weeks you've been as happy as I can ever remember."

"Hey," he said. "It's not like I was miserable before."

"Didn't say you were." She had a cup of tea next to her. She sipped some, then put the cup back down on the coffee table in front of her. "By the way? I thought the whole thing might turn out to be a disaster too. For everybody. But it's been the opposite. And I think it's been even better for your father than it's been for you. This whole experience has changed him."

"How?"

"Well, I could be the one making a joke, and say how comfortable he is finally hanging around with people his own age. But seriously? Being able to help you, and helping the team in the process—being a part of a team again—has made him think about somebody other than himself, which has been a full-time job for most of his life. All I know is, he's a lot happier person than he was when he left."

"Are you okay with all this?" Teddy said.

"*This?*"

"Me and Dad. Spending this much time together. Figuring it out."

She smiled.

"I am," she said. "I really am. And it's for one of the oldest reasons in the book. A boy does need his dad."

"I didn't believe that was true, you know."

"I'm not sure I did either."

She held up a finger, walked into the kitchen, and put on another mix of her music. When she came back, Teddy said to her, "Why *did* he leave?"

She paused and said, "Because I asked him to."

"*You* asked *him*?" Teddy said. He stared at her. "I always thought it was his idea."

"Right after it was mine."

"Why didn't you ever tell me that?"

"Because it was complicated, honey. Because divorce usually is."

"I'm a smart guy," Teddy said.

She leaned forward, elbows on knees. She was smiling again. "I don't want to be quoted on this," she said. "But I didn't want to be a mother to both of you."

"I don't understand," Teddy said.

"Neither did I for a long time," she said.

"You're saying you needed to take care of Dad?"

"A lot," she said. "There's a lot going on with him on the other side of that smile, Teddy. Even you must have figured that out by now, as much time as the two of you have spent together."

"All I've been able to figure out," Teddy said, "is that it still makes him sad, having football taken away from him the way it was."

She sipped her tea. "He's never tried to keep that a secret," she said. "But I do think that's why he's enjoying himself right now, because it *is* a way for him to go back to the days before he got hurt. And maybe live out his dreams all over again through you."

"I don't even know what my dreams are!" Teddy said.

"Maybe they're not the same ones," she said. "But I'll bet they're close enough, especially now that you're a quarterback. This whole season is like one great big do-over for him."

"You're the one who keeps telling me he never really wanted to grow up, right?" Teddy said.

"And this season he doesn't have to."

The assembly for *The Voice* was loud and fun. The kids in the gym got into it as much as the singers did, which made Teddy and the other coaches wonder how big and loud and fun the finals were going to be next week.

Teddy wasn't any kind of music expert, even having gone through the competition, but he thought the band that Mrs. Brandon had hired was really good. And Mrs. Brandon decided to act as master of ceremonies herself. She interviewed the singers before they each did their numbers and had them explain why they'd chosen the songs they had.

Katie went first, and even if you didn't know much about music, you knew that she had killed it. Her song was "Sugar" by Maroon 5, and when she finished, she got a long standing ovation from the crowd.

Teddy turned to Gus and said, "If she doesn't make the finals, it will be a bigger upset than me ending up playing quarter-back."

The kids were still cheering Katie. Cassie stood up and did the same. When she sat down, she looked at the other coaches and said, "You're all toast, no matter who ends up going against us in the finals."

"So the semis are already over?" Jack said.

"So over," Cassie said.

"And by the way?" Teddy said. "Whoever goes up against 'us' in the finals? Which part of Katie's song did you sing?"

"It's all in the coaching," Cassie said. "That poor girl could hardly sing a note before me."

Gregg Leonard, Teddy's guy, was next. It was still amazing to Teddy that Gregg had put himself out there this way. He couldn't stop thinking of Gregg as the centerfielder on their baseball team, or the Wildcats' safety and punter. But the guy could sing. Mrs. Brandon kept telling them to stop acting so surprised, constantly mocking the idea that being a singer somehow made him less of a jock.

Today he got the crowd going by putting on a big Pharrell Williams hat right before he started. Then he bounced all over the stage as he sang "Happy" from the movie *Despicable Me 2*. If he was intimidated by having to follow what Katie had just done, he didn't show it.

He killed it too. When he finished, Teddy jumped off from the coaches' table and nearly knocked him over with a high five. When he came back, he pointed at Cassie and said, "You know who's happy right now? Coach Teddy, that's who!"

Jack's singer, Vi, did a good job with her Taylor Swift song. And Angela Morales, Teddy had to admit, did a decent job herself with Beyoncé's song "Irreplaceable." But you could tell by the reaction from the crowd that it was game over.

When the kids had filed into the gym, they'd been given cards for Coach Teddy, Coach Cassie, Coach Jack, and Coach Gus. Each kid in the gym got to vote for two singers after Angela had finished her song. They passed the cards to the ends of their rows, and the kids from Mrs. B's music class collected them. The music kids then handed them to the teacher, who would go backstage and count the votes, while the band played a couple of songs.

When they finished, Teddy's mom brought an envelope out to Mrs. Brandon. She asked the four singers to come back up onstage. When she opened the envelope, she nodded her head and waited, letting the tension build a little more.

"And the finalists are . . . Katie and Gregg!" she said into her microphone, as the crowd in the gym went crazy for both of them all over again. In that moment, Teddy knew what it must feel like when a coach watched his team win a big game. He was sure Cassie felt the same way.

The bell rang then. The kids in the gym folded their chairs and stacked them against the wall before they all exited the gym.

"Katie is so winning this," Cassie said to Teddy backstage.

Teddy's mom was with them.

"Just remember that we're all trying to win something here," she said.

"We know, Mom," Teddy said. "And if we don't make enough money, then we lose, and so does the school."

"Amen," Alexis Madden said.

"That sounds like a prayer," Cassie said.

"You better believe it," Teddy's mom said to her. "Maybe this has been a Hail Mary pass from the start."

It had been too good a day, they'd all had too much fun, for Teddy to point out to her how rarely passes like those were completed.

TWENTY-SEVEN

If they beat the Brenham Bengals on Saturday, on the road, the Wildcats were one win away from a spot in the league championship game.

It meant they were three games away from being undefeated league champions.

And they were one more win after that from playing their way to MetLife Stadium.

Teddy didn't talk about this stuff in front of Jack. By now

he knew how big Jack was—how *fixed* he was, even though he hadn't played since their first game of the season—on not getting ahead of yourself in sports.

But how can I not get ahead of myself?

He had told his mother he wasn't sure he understood his own football dreams, just because the whole season, at least so far, had been like one crazy dream. Sometimes it seemed like just a couple of days ago that he'd needed to make that great, Beckham-like catch just to make the team as a tight end.

Now things had turned out pretty good for him. No, that wasn't quite accurate. Things had turned out great for him, better than he ever could have imagined. And things really were better with his dad than he ever could have hoped for that first day.

His dad *had* helped him become a real quarterback, even if Teddy still thought of himself as just holding Jack's place. He was all right with that. He was. In his heart, as much fun as it had been to learn how to play quarterback and then play it as decently as he had, he still wanted to be Beckham.

It didn't mean he wasn't proud of what he'd accomplished, even if there was still a long way to go. He remembered something Coach Gilbert had told them before the season started.

"I want every one of you to make me proud this season," he said. "But more than that, I want you to make yourselves proud."

Tomorrow Teddy just wanted to keep this roll they were on going against Brenham. He was in his bed, playbook on his lap. He'd been studying it for more than an hour, but he now felt all studied out. His dad had told him when he was dropping him off after practice tonight that could happen sometimes, no matter how well you wanted to prepare for a game and for an opponent. Sometimes you had to close the playbook and stop, because you felt as if you had *too* much information.

"Do you feel like you're still learning about the position?" Teddy said before he got out of his dad's car.

He saw his dad smile. It wasn't the big smile he put on for the world, the one Teddy was used to by now, what he thought of as his dad's salesman smile. This one was different.

This one seemed to come straight from his heart.

"I'm still learning *period*," his dad said.

There was a lot he still wasn't sure of with his dad, a lot about him he felt like he didn't know, even a lot he still didn't trust. He wasn't even willing to admit that he loved his dad, or would ever love him the way Gus loved his dad, or Jack loved his. Or Cassie loved hers. He wasn't sure, even with what his mom had told him, if he could ever be able to forgive his dad for being away as long as he was; if he'd be able to forgive *or* forget.

He was pretty sure that as good as things might get between

him and his dad, he'd never love him the way he loved his mom, who'd always been there for him.

There was a lot to this story he hadn't figured out yet.

But this much he did know about his dad:

He was definitely getting to like him. For now, that seemed like more than enough.

TWENTY-EIGHT

Maybe he had gotten so fixed on an undefeated season in their league that he *had* looked past the Brenham Bengals, who'd won only one game.

Or maybe it wasn't anything more complicated than Teddy being due for a bad game. He watched enough pro football on television to know that even the great ones threw in a stinker once in a while, sometimes when you least expected it.

But Teddy wasn't just having a bad game. He was having

his worst, against the worst team in the league.

On the Wildcats' first drive, a long one, he fumbled on the Bengals' one yard line. He had gotten stopped short of the goal line but reached out with the ball, thinking he could get it across the line before his knee touched. While he was doing that, the Bengals' middle linebacker just slapped the ball away and recovered it himself.

The Wildcats' defense managed to keep the Bengals pinned down there and forced them to punt from their own end zone. So Teddy and the guys on offense started their second drive of the game on Brenham's twenty-nine yard line. But that drive, if you could even call it that, lasted just two plays. Teddy tried to force a pass into Gus, then watched helplessly as the cornerback covering Gus timed his move perfectly, stepped in front of Gus, intercepted the ball, and took off down the sideline. Teddy was the Wildcat closest to him, but had no shot at catching the kid before he turned the play into an easy pick six.

The defense stuffed the conversion, a run up the middle, but the damage was done. It was 6–0 for the home team.

Teddy's dad tried to console him on the sideline. But Teddy didn't want to be consoled. He was way too angry at himself over what had just happened on the field.

"Lot of football to be played," his dad said. "A *lot*."

"Yeah, a lot of bad football if I keep going like this."

"You won't."

"You don't know that!" Teddy said. "I know you know a lot about playing quarterback, but you don't know everything!"

He started to walk away, to get a drink and try to calm himself down. His dad stopped him by putting a hand on his shoulder. "I'm trying to help you."

"I get it," Teddy said. "But you can't play for me. I gotta figure this out myself."

Now his dad put hands on both of Teddy's shoulders and turned him around so they were facing each other. "You need to listen even if you don't want to. If you start pressing after you make a couple of mistakes, all that does is produce *more* mistakes. That fumble happened because you were trying to make a play. That wasn't a bad thing, you just pulled a bad result." He smiled. "Now the throw you just made, I can't lie, that was god-awful."

"Thanks for sharing, Dad. I hadn't picked up on that myself."

"But everybody makes bad throws! Look at the throw Russell Wilson made that time when the Seahawks blew it against the Patriots. And that happened in the last minute of the Super Bowl! You've got all day to make up for your lousy throw. Okay?"

He was right. Teddy knew he was right. "Okay," he said.

"Now go get a drink," his dad said. "And when you get back out there, just tell yourself that you're starting the game all over again, and that all we've done is spot those guys one score."

But he *was* still pressing when he got back out there. He missed throws that he'd been making all season, that he thought he could make in his sleep. Because he was missing, the Bengals started putting more and more guys in the box, stopping Jake and Brian when the Wildcats tried to run the ball, almost daring Teddy to find his form throwing the ball.

But he couldn't, at least not consistently. This close to a perfect ending to their season, it was like he was all the way back at the beginning and had never played a game at quarterback in his life.

It was still 6–0 at the half. The second time the Wildcats got the ball in the third quarter, Teddy got sacked and fumbled again, again deep in Bengals territory. He'd made some decent throws getting his team down there. But all he had to show was another wasted drive.

Once again the Wildcats' defense picked him up, forcing the Bengals into a quick three-and-out. It was starting to look as if their opponents were never going to score an offensive touchdown, not the way Max Conte and Andre Williams and Gregg Leonard were flying around the field. But Teddy really was starting to wonder, the way he was playing, if he was capable of putting any points on the board himself.

Jack kept trying to pump him up on the sideline, the same way Gus and Teddy's dad were. Nothing was working. And the clock kept running.

"Remember way back at the beginning, when I told you to trust your arm?" Jack said as the two teams changed sides to start the fourth quarter. "This would be a good time to try that."

"It's not just my arm!" Teddy said. "I'm not trusting *me*."

They were sitting next to each other on the bench. When the quarter started, it would be Brenham's ball, second down, their own forty.

"You sound like a loser," Jack said in a voice only loud enough for Teddy to hear. "That's not you."

"But we *are* losing," Teddy said. "And I'm the biggest reason we are."

"You need to start thinking about how you're going to win the game," Jack said.

"Maybe I don't know how to do that today."

"I'm sorry. Did the game just end, or the third quarter?"

"It just might not be my day," Teddy said.

"If you really feel that way, I've got nothing." Jack stood up. "You sound like you've given up."

"Wait," Teddy said. "I promise to stop whining. Tell me what I need to do to turn this around before it's too late."

"You *know* what to do. Forget what's gone wrong so far. Remember all the plays you've made this season, and go make a few more. That's what I always try to do."

"I'm not you."

"Yeah, well, I'd rather be you today," Jack said. "Because you've still got a game to play."

The Bengals ran their best drive of the game once the quarter started, and ran off a lot of clock in the process, making one third down play after another. All Teddy could do was stand and watch from the sideline. They finally ended up at the Wildcats' eleven. But then their quarterback was the one being the drive killer.

He waited too long to pitch the ball on the option play they'd been running for most of the drive. When he did get rid of the ball, Max Conte was right there and tried to launch him into outer space. The Bengals' quarterback went flying in one direction, the ball went flying in another. Max recovered it. The Wildcats had the ball back at their own fifteen.

Four and a half minutes left.

They needed a score, and then a conversion. They had to get a win, not a tie. In Teddy's mind, a real unbeaten record didn't have a tie on it.

There was a delay on the field, because one of the Bengals'

offensive linemen was being helped to his feet by his teammates. Teddy turned and took a look up into the stands, where his mom was standing along with the other Walton parents. One more time this season, it was as if she was waiting for him to look up there. As soon as he did, she gave him the signal she always did: she pounded her heart twice. Teddy did the same.

"Hey."

It was his dad.

"Trust your arm," he said.

"You sound like Jack."

"Great minds," his dad said.

"Jack said he'd give anything to be me right now."

His dad grinned. "So would I."

Then his dad said, "When you get out there, short post slot."

"Got it."

It was a pass over the middle to Gus, maybe ten yards up the field. Teddy knew there would be traffic. There always was when you threw into the belly of the defense trying to make a play. He nearly threw the ball too hard—and nearly too high— as Gus broke free, wanting to make sure only Gus had a chance to catch it. But Gus went up and got it, and secured possession before he hit the ground. First down.

Teddy threw it again on the next play, a short, safe pass to Nate Vinton in the flat. The Wildcats gained eight more yards.

Jake ran for a first down. Just like that, they were out to their forty.

Three minutes left.

Teddy knew they weren't playing for their season. They could tie or lose today and still make the championship game. But it still felt as if this game was everything. Maybe it was because he'd played so badly for most of the game. Maybe that was why he wanted this game so badly.

He missed Gus on first down. But he came right back to him on second, a twelve-yard completion to the left sideline, the Wildcats' side of the field, stopping the clock. Under two minutes. But they were in Bengals' territory.

Jake ran it. Brian ran it. The Wildcats had another first down. Now they were inside the Bengals' forty. Teddy threw the best ball he had all day to Mike O'Keeffe, deep down the middle. The Bengals finally brought Mike down at the fifteen.

Coach Gilbert called time-out.

The clock showed a minute and thirty left.

"You're hot now," Coach Gilbert said to Teddy.

"It had to happen eventually," Teddy said, grinning. "Law of averages."

Coach Gilbert nodded at Teddy's dad. "We think it's a perfect time for a quarterback draw."

"But to make it work, you've got to sell it better than you

have all season, starting with when you drop back," Teddy's dad said. "Get that ball up on your shoulder right away, like you are throwing all the way. Then stop and run right behind Charlie Lyons's big old butt."

"I won't tell Charlie that part," Teddy said.

"One other thing?" his dad said.

"Hold on to the ball?"

His dad pointed at him. "There you go."

They used a formation where Mike O'Keeffe, their tight end, moved outside, making it a three-wideout look. It was another way of selling the idea that they were throwing. The Brenham middle linebacker shaded toward Mike and away from the middle. It would give Teddy some room to run, if he could get there.

Teddy went with a long count, stepped back from center, and set the ball on his right shoulder. Ahead of him he saw Charlie Lyons clear out the Brenham nose tackle.

After a three-step drop, Teddy pulled the ball down and ran.

He was already at the ten, with more open field in front of him, before linebackers started coming at him from both sides. But they were late, behind him, trying to catch up. By now Teddy was at full speed. He felt as if he were running downhill.

The last guy to beat was one of their safeties, at about the two yard line. Teddy didn't slow down, not wanting to bring the guys chasing back into the play. He simply lowered his shoulder and plowed right through the kid, until he was in the end zone standing up.

It was 6–6.

Teddy handed the ball to the ref and waved off Gus and Mike as they ran toward him, wanting to celebrate. Nothing to celebrate yet. There was still work to do. They still needed one more point to close the deal.

Brian brought the play in from the sideline.

"Roll option right," he said.

"Yes!" Gus Morales said, the word coming out of him like steam.

If he got open, the ball was coming to him. He would line up in the left slot. Teddy would roll to his right. Gus would cut all the way across the field, to the right corner of the end zone. He would be the only Wildcats receiver on that side of the field. If he was covered, Teddy had to find somebody all the way over on the left side, or run it himself.

"You be there," Teddy said to Gus.

"You get it there."

The outside linebacker to Teddy's right nearly blew up the play. He almost beat the snap count and was past Mike O'Keeffe before Mike could even think about putting a block on him, and then he was all over Teddy before he could even get to the outside.

But in that moment Teddy wasn't a quarterback. He was a tight end again, using his size and his strength to shed the kid as he tried to bring him down and keep the game tied.

He stumbled slightly as he got away. Somehow he managed to keep his balance as he kept moving to his right. As he did, he saw Gus clear his coverage.

He couldn't risk stopping to set his feet. Gus was too close to the sideline and too close to the back of the end zone.

Now.

Teddy, still on the move, slung the ball sidearm, trying to be as accurate as he could, trying to put the ball in a spot where only Gus had a chance to catch it. He was worried after he let the ball go that he might have led Gus too much; led him right off the field.

Only then Gus Morales was the one reaching out and trying to make a play. Teddy had led him too much, but not so much that Gus couldn't catch his fingertips on the ball and pull it close to him, managing to keep both feet inbounds as he did. The ref's arms shot up in the air. The Wildcats had their point.

Three plays later Henry Koepp intercepted a desperation throw from the Bengals' quarterback.

Teddy ran back onto the field. He took two knees. The game was over. Wildcats 7, Bengals 6. When the ref blew his whistle, Teddy ran right for Jack Callahan.

"You were right!" he yelled. "The game wasn't over!"

Jack smiled.

"Well, it is now," he said.

TWENTY-NINE

I t had turned into the most exciting week of Teddy's life, on
and off the field.

There was Saturday's game against the Greenacres Giants,
who had one loss and were tied with Norris in second place.
But because the possibility of Greenacres beating them and
Norris winning its last regular season game set up the possibility of a three-way tie for first, the Wildcats-Giants game was
the same as a play-off game.

Coach Gilbert had told them the night before at practice that the board members running the league didn't want to push back the championship game, not with the county championship already scheduled in two weeks. So they'd brought the three coaches in and had them flip coins, just in case there was a three-way tie.

And Coach had lost the coin flip. "First thing we've lost all season," he told the team. "So we better keep winning."

The game against Greenacres was a win-or-go-home game. It was like they were playing one championship game to get to another, and then another after that, if they wanted to make it to MetLife Stadium.

It almost made Teddy glad he had *The Voice* to at least take his mind off football.

Teddy hadn't done any coaching about singing with Gregg Leonard, his guy in the competition, from the start. He hadn't talked about what songs Gregg should pick or anything like that. The best he could do was treat it like sports and continue to give Gregg coaching advice. Mostly it was about trusting his talent, and telling him that this was a different way of trying to make a play to win a big game, before they'd both get the chance to do the same thing against Greenacres.

His mom had been on fire all week and was even more

crazed now that it was Thursday and the big night had finally arrived. Teddy had shown up early with her and couldn't believe how cool the lobby of Walton Middle looked, all these tables set up with silent auction items that school parents and their friends and local businesspeople had donated as a way of raising even more money than they already had. There were tickets to Patriots games and Red Sox games and the use of a private suite for a Giants game at MetLife Stadium and even a trip to the Bahamas somebody had donated just the day before.

"Some of this stuff is amazing," Teddy said.

"It is," his mom said. "But people better come up big, because we're still not there."

As they got closer to the start of the show, his mom kept going back and forth from the stage to the lobby every few minutes. She said she was pretty sure they were going to have a sellout, that she wasn't worried about that; she had a good idea of the amount of money ticket sales were going to bring in. Now she needed those auction items to come through for her.

"You keep saying we're going to be short," Teddy said backstage.

He was wearing his blazer and a tie and khaki pants and loafers. All the judges were dressed up. Cassie was wearing a new dress her mother had bought her for the occasion.

"I'm better at math than you are," his mom said, taking another peek through the curtains.

"Ouch."

"Tonight is all-or-nothing," she said. "The town won't extend the deadline. If we do come up short when we total up the money, then everything we've raised goes to Walton Middle for its new fields project, and there's no music department next semester."

"Our fields are fine, by the way."

"Tell our town that," she said.

"So people have to come up big at the auction?" Teddy said.

"They have to come up *huge*."

"You're the one who keeps telling us that it's never over till it's over," Teddy said. "Or until the fat lady sings."

That at least got a grin out of his mom. "Well," she said, "the singing is about to begin, isn't it?"

The time came to close the auction. Before his mom walked back to the lobby, she said to him, "Your dad is here, by the way."

It surprised Teddy. "He is?"

"He said that if I could go to your games, he could come to mine," she said.

Then she was gone. Teddy peeked through the curtains and watched her walk down the middle aisle, waving at friends who were already in their seats.

Fifteen minutes later, it was showtime.

He wanted this for Gregg, because he knew how hard Gregg had worked, and he couldn't imagine the pressure of performing in front of this many adults. He wanted this for Mrs. Brandon, because he knew how hard *she'd* worked, and he'd come to understand that she did love her music as much as he and his friends loved their sports.

But he was surprised, now that the show was starting, how much he wanted this for his mom.

It felt as good as she said it would doing something for somebody else:

Her.

It was a great show.

The band had added a couple of members, which made the music sound better than ever. The two losing semifinalists, Vi and Angela, sang a duet. Some of the girls from Mrs. Brandon's chorale sang two songs. After they did, Mrs. B came back out and thanked everybody for their support all over again.

Teddy's mom had been right about the crowd: the gym was completely full. They'd even had to roll out bleachers on one side to handle the overflow. Maybe his mom wouldn't need as much money from the auction as she thought. Maybe, he thought, they'd get their happy ending after all.

Even here they'd used a coin flip, to determine which of the finalists would go first. Katie won the toss and said she'd rather go last. Gregg had told Teddy that if he could play baseball in the Little League World Series on ESPN, he could get through tonight. But Teddy still watched in awe as he walked to the microphone and proceeded to belt out Justin Timberlake's song "Mirrors."

Gregg got a standing ovation. As he did, Teddy and Cassie turned their backs to him, just like the coaches did on *The Voice*. As Gregg walked off the stage, he leaned down and said into Teddy's ear, "I won't be as happy if I win as I am that I'm done!"

It was Katie's turn. She had picked a Katy Perry song, "Roar." When she was done, and the people in the gym jumped to their feet and roared for her, Cassie didn't turn around this time. She jumped up from her seat and ran across the stage and hugged Katie.

When she came back to their small table, Teddy said, "I thought I was going to have to flag you for excessive celebration."

The people were still applauding. Over the continuing roar of the crowd, Cassie yelled, "I'll take the fifteen yards!"

The band played a couple of songs while the votes were counted. Mrs. Brandon came out for the big moment, an envelope in her hand. She opened it up and smiled as she looked at the card she'd just pulled out. Then she announced that Katie Cummings had won.

Jack and Gus brought out the trophy from behind the curtain. Katie went back to the microphone and thanked Mrs. Brandon and Teddy's mom and Cassie. She congratulated Gregg, right before she said she was donating the hundred dollars she'd won as champion to what she called "the Mrs. B fund."

Mrs. Brandon took the microphone from her and said, "This was never about me. It wasn't just Katie who won tonight. The music won." That got the people cheering again.

With the show nearly over, Teddy looked across the stage at his mom. She had a card in her hand too. And despite all the noise and excitement in the gym, and talk about winners, she looked totally defeated.

Then somebody was standing next to her: his dad. He put his arm around her, said something into her ear, and began walking out onto the stage, making Teddy wonder if another show was about to begin.

THIRTY

Teddy looked out at the audience. The people were just waiting, probably thinking this *was* part of the show.

Cassie leaned over and whispered in his ear. "What's he doing?"

"Not a clue."

Teddy looked back at his mom. He tried to read her face now. But he couldn't. She was just one more person in the gym waiting to see—and hear—what was about to happen.

"I'm David Madden," his dad said. "I see a lot of familiar faces in this crowd. But the best way for me to introduce myself, at least the way one football season is going in this town, is as Teddy Madden's dad."

He turned and smiled at Teddy. Teddy gave a quick wave toward the audience, just because he felt as if he ought to do something.

"Of course you all know Teddy's mom," his dad continued, "because she is the person who did the most to make this night happen, along with our wonderful champion, Katie, and all the other people who performed on this stage. Why don't we give everybody involved one more round of applause?"

He did, and they did. Cassie leaned over again and said to Teddy, "I thought Mrs. Brandon was the emcee."

"Not anymore," Teddy said.

"We all know why we're here tonight," Teddy's dad said, "and the way we voted not just for Katie and Gregg, but with our wallets."

He paused, to let that sink in.

"Anyway, Teddy's mom was just handed the final numbers raised by this event. And, sadly, it turns out that we've come up short of the figure needed to keep Mrs. Brandon's music department, which she loves, up and running at a school that she loves."

No cheering in the gym now. Just a collective groan.

"Where's he going with this?" Cassie said.

"Why don't we both be quiet and find out?"

She didn't punch him this time. She kicked him under the table.

He had to hand it to his dad. Whatever was coming next, he was milking it for all it was worth. Then his dad reached into the inside pocket of his blazer and came out with a check. He held up the check so the people in the audience could see.

"I just covered the difference," David Madden said. "All the people who put on this wonderful show have come too far to be stopped at the one yard line."

He turned now toward Teddy's mom. "Alexis, please come out here so I can hand you this check," he said.

As she did, the crowd jumped to its feet once more with an ovation to rock the gym one last time. Teddy's mom looked embarrassed as his dad handed her the check. But she smiled as she accepted it.

Teddy wondered how she felt now that her moment had become his.

"What just happened here?" Cassie said to Teddy.

"My dad's the one who ended up throwing the Hail Mary pass," he said. "Completed it too."

THIRTY-ONE

It was an hour before the Walton-Greenacres game at Holzman Field. Teddy and Gus were stretching on the field along with their teammates.

Teddy's dad hadn't arrived yet, but when Teddy looked over to the sideline, he saw Jack standing with Coach Gilbert and Coach Williams. Why not? Jack had been acting like an assistant coach from the time he got hurt.

Behind them the bleachers were already starting to fill up.

Cassie and Kate and Angela were sitting in the front row, laughing about something. The day at Holzman was beginning to take shape.

"No way Norris loses to Brenham today," Gus said.

"We just gotta keep winning," Teddy said.

"Still doesn't seem right, losing a coin flip being this big a deal after we haven't lost a stupid game."

"It won't matter," Teddy said, "because we're not losing this game."

"That's why they made you quarterback," Gus said. "The way you can break things down like that."

They were done stretching. When Teddy stood up, he looked around again, wanting to take it all in, because a part of him—a big part—still didn't believe that he was the quarterback of this team, and that he was here.

Maybe they would have still gotten to this day undefeated with somebody else at quarterback. Maybe the Wildcats were just that good. But he'd never know that, and neither would his teammates.

"Even though there's no script in sports," Coach Gilbert had been telling Teddy and Jack just the other night after practice, "there's always a reason why things happen the way they do. Who steps up in the big moment, who doesn't. Who's there, who's not."

Teddy walked over to the bench and picked up a ball, then waved at his receivers to follow him toward the ten yard line at this end of the field. Then Gus and Mike and Nate and Jake and Brian took turns running some simple pass routes, like now they were beginning to stretch out the Wildcats' passing game. Charlie Lyons joined them after a few minutes, direct-snapping some balls to Teddy before they switched to a shotgun formation.

The Giants were at the other end of the field, their quarterback going through the same progressions Teddy was. Greenacres was more than an hour away, but Teddy could see from the bleachers on the other side of the field that they had brought a lot of fans with them.

Jack came out and stood next to Teddy.

"Is this where you give me my pregame pep talk?" Teddy said.

"Nope. You don't need one today."

"It should be you out here throwing the ball around. You know that, right?"

"Nope," Jack said again. "This is your team now. Like your dad says. Stuff happens for a reason."

"I hear you," Teddy said. "Like there was a reason why my dad came back."

He told Jack to go out for a pass now, threw him a beauty

over the middle. Then he walked toward the sideline, as ready as he was ever going to be.

That was when he saw his mom standing behind their bench, waving at him. He grinned as he got closer to her, seeing that she already had her game face on.

"Hey," he said. "Shouldn't you be up in your lucky spot by now?"

"Teddy," she said, "there's no easy way to tell you this."

"Tell me what?"

"Your father's not coming today."

"That's not funny," he said.

He'd been so busy focusing on his pregame routine that he hadn't looked for his father in the past few minutes. But he looked over his shoulder now, to where Coach Gilbert and Coach Williams and Jack were looking at the play sheet in Coach Gilbert's hand.

No sign of his dad anywhere.

"Maybe he's just late," Teddy said, turning back to his mom.

"Teddy, listen to me," she said. "He's not coming. He left early this morning, while you were still sleeping, for California. I hadn't checked my phone for messages until I got to the field. I couldn't quite understand him, but he said it was business."

"But . . . it's the biggest game of the year," Teddy said.

He was afraid his mom might cry. Teddy knew the feeling.

"I waited until you stopped practicing," she said. "I told Coach Gilbert. He thought I should be the one to tell you."

Teddy just stood there, feeling his head start to spin, wanting to go sit down on the bench. He didn't know what to say, or what he was supposed to do next. All he knew was that the game was starting in a few minutes, with or without his dad, a game his team needed to win, even if Teddy had already lost something before it began.

His dad had left him.

Again.

THIRTY-TWO

Teddy's mom told him to just try to clear his head and go win the game; that was the most important thing right now.

"Not for him," Teddy said.

"Just control what *you* can control," she said.

Then she added, "Love you."

"Love you, too."

He walked over to where Coach Gilbert and Jack and Gus were waiting for him, thinking that he really shouldn't be surprised. He should have expected this all along.

Coach Gilbert put an arm around him. "Listen, I know how disappointed you must be. I'm a little disappointed in him too, not gonna lie. I just want you to know that I've got your back today. So do your teammates."

"So do I," Jack said.

"So do I," Gus Morales said. "We still got this, right?"

"Oh, we got this all right," Teddy said.

He wished he were as sure of that as he sounded.

Jared Stadler, the Giants' quarterback, had the best arm Teddy had seen on an opposing quarterback all season and was showing it off on his team's first drive of the game. Jared threw on all but two of the plays and missed only one open receiver. He finally hit his slot guy for a twenty-yard touchdown pass and followed that by connecting with his tight end for the conversion. It was 7–0, Giants. The whole drive had taken just three minutes.

"Okay, now it's our turn," Coach Gilbert said to Teddy. "We don't have to get even all at once. Let's just run out stuff, mix it up with runs and passes like we have all season."

"Okay," Teddy said.

"You okay?"

"Please don't keep asking me that the whole game, Coach."

Teddy didn't throw his first pass until Jake and Brian had

gotten the Wildcats two first downs pounding the middle of the Giants' line. They were at the Giants' forty-eight by then. But Teddy overthrew Mike O'Keeffe on first down, before doing the same to Gus on second, even though Gus nearly made an impossible catch on the left sideline.

Coach Gilbert, calling all the plays now, tried to fool the Giants on third-and-ten with a draw to Jake. But they didn't fool the Giants' middle linebacker, who stopped Jake at the line for no gain. Gregg Leonard punted the ball away. The Giants took over on their twenty-five. On first down Jared Stadler threw the ball as far as he could down the middle of the field to his fastest wide receiver. Gregg read the play perfectly and came over to help out on the coverage. He timed his jump perfectly but couldn't get high enough to get two hands on the ball. He ended up tipping the ball forward. It fell right into the hands of the Giants' receiver, like the play had been designed that way. The kid ran the rest of the way untouched. Max Conte broke up the conversion pass to the same kid. But it was still 13–0, Giants. The first quarter was only half over, and Teddy felt as if he hadn't even been in the game yet.

"They're gonna score every time they have the ball," Teddy said to Jack.

"You know," Jack said, "that hardly ever happens in football."

"First time for everything."

"Tell me something," Jack said.

"What?"

"What's your absolute favorite pass play?"

"That crossing pattern, off the option, the one we used to beat Brenham."

"Go tell Coach you want to run that on first down."

"So now you're the new offensive coordinator?" Teddy said.

Jack grinned at him, then shrugged. "Well," he said, "somebody's gotta be."

Teddy told Coach what Jack had said, and what he wanted to run.

"Go for it," Coach said. "What's your second favorite pattern?"

"Curl to Mike."

"Run that after you hit Gus. If this is gonna be a shoot-out, I guess we need to start firing back."

Teddy made the throw to Gus. He hit Mike on the curl. *Now* he was in the game. Coach let him keep throwing. There was a screen to Jake. A pass in the right flat to Brian. He hit Nate over the middle for ten more yards, before they ran a neat pick play to Gus. Nate ran into Gus's area as if he were the intended receiver again, even waving for the ball. Gus snuck right in behind him. Teddy hit him in stride. The field opened up as if half the Giants' defense had gone home, and Gus was a streak all the way to the end zone. Jake ran behind Charlie Lyons for the conversion. It was 13–7.

When Teddy got to the sideline, Jack threw him a serious high five.

"Don't hurt yourself," Teddy said.

"Oh, you got this all right," Jack said.

"*We* got it."

The Wildcats went on a long drive just before halftime, one of their longest of the year, starting at their own eight yard line and eating up nearly six minutes of clock. When they finally ended up with a first-and-goal from the Giants' eight, Teddy decided to fake it to Jake on the off-tackle play Coach had sent in, run the naked bootleg his dad liked so much to perfection, and beat everybody to the end zone. It was 13-all. He didn't have to like his dad today. It didn't mean he couldn't like his plays.

Their outside linebacker made a terrific play in front of Mike to knock down the conversion pass. The score was still 13-all, which was what it was when the half ended. They were either two quarters away from keeping their perfect season going, or they were two quarters away from going home. Both teams knew the league had decided no ties today. They'd play until they had a winner.

At halftime Cassie came down behind their bench. She was the one waving Teddy over. Once he got to her, she didn't waste any time getting to *it*.

"I heard," she said.

"I figure by now even people on Mars have heard."

"You good?" she said.

"I'm good."

"I know you're *playing* good," she said. "But how are you?"

"Cass, can we talk about this after the game, please?" he said. "I know you're being my friend. But I've already figured out I don't miss him and I don't need him to win this game."

She smiled. "Then go kick some butt," she said.

She turned to leave.

"Cass?" he said.

She turned back around.

"Thanks," he said.

"For what?"

"For being here."

"Where else am I gonna be, you big dummy?" she said, and went to join her friends.

Teddy went and got a drink before taking a seat, alone, at the end of the bench. He knew he had been kidding Cassie, and kidding himself. He *did* miss having his dad on the sideline. Just as a coach, not anything else. His dad still saw things that nobody else saw, in the Wildcats' offense and the other team's defense. He still had the feel for the game that Coach Gilbert talked about.

But that didn't matter if you weren't *at* the game, if you had more important things to do on the day of a game like this for your son's team.

A team he said was his, too.

THIRTY-THREE

Right before the third quarter began, Coach Gilbert came and sat down next to Teddy.

"How we lookin'?" he said.

"I'm not ready for the season to end."

"Now that is amazing, like we are reading each other's minds! Because I feel the exact same way."

"We don't have to win a whole game now," Teddy said. "Just a half."

"Exactly," Coach said. "We've been the best team in this league all year. No reason why we can't be that for the next hour or so."

Max and Andre and Gregg, the three best players on the defense, came walking over to stand in front of them. Max did the talking. That figured. He was the one who did the most talking when the other team had the ball.

"We're not letting that quarterback beat us," Max said.

"That sounds like an *excellent* strategy!" Teddy said.

"What I'm saying," Max said, "is that they're not getting another score. That means you only have to get us one."

Teddy stood up. So did Coach. Somehow, in that moment, the whole team gathered around them. Teddy put his right hand in the air. The other guys did the same.

"Wildcats!" he yelled.

"*Wildcats!*" they all yelled back, like they wanted to be heard on Mars.

The game slowed down then, as if the stakes today, what they were all playing for, had hit them even harder than when the game had started. It was as if the offensive players had started to worry that one mistake might cost their team its season. More than once Teddy couldn't help himself: he wondered what the game plan would be if his dad were here, wondered if he'd be taking more chances.

MIKE LUPICA

The Wildcats got past midfield just one time in the third quarter. The Giants didn't get past midfield until halfway through the fourth quarter. The Wildcats had to punt the ball away with six minutes to go, deep into Giants' territory. Jared completed a couple of passes, but then Max Conte blew past everybody and sacked him on third down. Jared, who also punted for his team, had to kick the ball away.

Three minutes left. There was an officials' time-out because of a problem with the game clock. Coach Gilbert came over and put an arm around Teddy's shoulders.

"This is all we could have asked for," Coach said, "a chance to be the team with the ball last and win the game."

Teddy took a deep breath. "Then let us try to win it," he said.

"What do you mean?"

"Stop calling the game like you're afraid to lose," Teddy said.

Coach took his arm away and got in front of Teddy. But he was smiling.

"Is that what you think I've been doing?"

"Yes."

Coach took a deep breath and let it out. "Even I forget sometimes that it's your game to win or lose, not mine."

"Put the game in my hands," Teddy said.

"I knew another quarterback who used to tell our coach the same thing."

THE EXTRA YARD

"I can do this," Teddy said. "*We* can do this."

The scoreboard operator fixed the clock problem. One of the refs came over and said, "Good to go, Dick."

"Slant to Gus," Coach said to Teddy. "Screen to Jake after that. Post to Gus after that."

Teddy nodded. "I won't let you down."

"Haven't yet, kid," Coach Gilbert said, and gave him a shove toward the field.

The slant got them eight yards. The screen got them five more. First down. Gus put a sweet move on the kid covering him, got an inside shoulder on him, got into the clear. Teddy threw him a smoking-hot ball. Gus covered up before he got hit. They were at the Giants' twenty, clock running. *Fine with me,* Teddy thought. *Let it run.*

He shot a quick look at the sideline. Coach Gilbert just stood there with his arms folded in front of him. Jake was next to him but made no move to bring in the next play. Coach unfolded his arms now and pointed at Teddy.

Like he was telling him, *Your call.*

He knelt in the huddle, looked up at the guys, and said, "Reverse pitch."

"Oh baby," Gus said.

The play called for a fake handoff to Brian, which Teddy knew had to be stellar, as both of them moved to their right.

Then Teddy would pull the ball back and pitch it to Gus, coming behind them, running the other way.

Gus was at full speed when he caught the ball. As soon as he was outside the line, he read the blocking and the defense perfectly and made a sharp inside cut. One of the Giants' safeties finally brought him down at the ten yard line.

Now Coach ran Jake into the game. When he got to the huddle, Teddy said, "Got a play for me?"

"Nope. Coach just told me to tell you it's all you now. 'Your game,' is what he said."

Teddy nodded, leaned into the huddle, and said, "Fake reverse."

It was basically the same play. Only instead of pitching the ball to Gus, Teddy was going to keep it and try to get to the outside, maybe all the way to the pylon.

"It's like we're playing behind your house," Gus said.

"Yeah," Teddy said. "Fun, huh?"

This time Teddy's best fake was to Gus. Then he pulled the ball down, and the Giants didn't put him down until he was at the three yard line. Coach called time.

Fifty seconds left.

Teddy ran to the sideline. When he got there, Jack handed him his water bottle. Coach waited until Teddy took a quick drink before he said, "You can tell me what you want to run," he said, "or I can be surprised along with everybody else."

Teddy told him the play he wanted to call. He was the quarterback of the Wildcats now, as much as he'd ever been. But he wanted Coach to know he still had a ton of tight end in him.

"Love it," Coach said.

"Me too," Jack said.

Teddy tossed his bottle back to Jack. He ran back onto the field, got in the huddle, and told the guys what they were running. He took the snap from Charlie and rolled to his right.

But then, at the last second, he pitched the ball to Jake, who had the only blocker he needed out in front of him:

Teddy Madden.

The only Greenacres kid with a chance to break up the play was their left outside linebacker. Teddy lowered his shoulder and bounced the kid halfway out of the end zone. Jake could have walked in behind him for the score. Wildcats 19, Giants 13. Teddy threw a perfect fade, just over the defense, to Gus in the right corner. Now it was 20–13.

Jared completed one pass to midfield, just to make the last half minute interesting. After that Gus, put in by Coach as an extra defensive back, intercepted a heave deep down the middle of the field. Teddy came back out to kneel one time. They were more a team today than they'd ever been, even if

MIKE LUPICA

they were down a former assistant coach. Now they were in the championship game.

"You do know," Coach Gilbert said when it was over, "that your dad got himself hurt throwing a block like that one time."

"Yeah," Teddy said. "He told me."

"You're not afraid of very much, are you?" Coach said.

Teddy looked up at him and said, "Not of getting hurt."

Then he went to go find his mom.

THIRTY-FOUR

A half hour after they'd gotten home from Holzman Field, his mom came into his room with a paper in her hand.

"This e-mail was waiting for me when I checked my laptop," she said. "Your dad asked me to print it out for you. He said that he was afraid if he sent it directly to you, you might delete it."

"One more good call by Dad."

"According to the time it was sent, he must have written it on the plane."

"You can do that?"

"A lot of planes have Wi-Fi now," she said. She reached out with the paper. At first Teddy made no move to take it from her.

"You should read it, Teddy," she said.

"Why?"

"He tells why he had to leave the way he did," she said. "Or at least why he thinks he had to leave the way he did."

He reluctantly took the paper. His mom left the room, closing the door behind her. Teddy held the paper, not looking at it, for what felt like a long time, before he finally began to read.

Dear Teddy,

I'm so sorry to have missed the game today. By the time you read this (if you're reading this), I'm just going to assume you did enough to play the 'Cats into the championship game.

I wish I could have explained everything to you before I left for the airport at dawn this morning. But everything happened pretty fast late last night, and I wasn't going to wake you up and have you lose sleep before the big game.

I'll try not to bore you with too many details. And at this point you probably don't care very much about them, anyway. But two job opportunities just happened to come my way in the last couple of weeks. One is in television, with Fox Sports in L.A., and the other is with the Chargers in San Diego. I promise you I didn't go looking for them, but once they just sort of found me, I felt I owed myself the chance to at least hear what people in both places had to say.

I don't expect you to understand, or feel sorry for me, but I just felt like this might be my last opportunity to have to stop smiling at people for a living, and kissing up to them, and trying to sell them things, starting with selling them me.

The TV job is in production, something I've always wanted to try. I think I even mentioned that I wanted to be a boss when I took you and your friends on that tour of ESPN. The opening with the Chargers is vice president in charge of marketing. It would be my chance to finally work in football. It would be marketing. I'd still be a boss.

The interview with the Chargers isn't until later this week. But the man interviewing me for Fox was leaving tonight for Australia and won't be back for over a month. He wanted to have one face-to-face interview with me before he left. So I had to take the first flight out this morning, because he had interviewed everybody else that he was considering except me,

MIKE LUPICA

and he wanted to make his decision before he came back.

I know I said I wouldn't leave you again. And you have to believe this has nothing to do with how much I love you, or how much I want you in my life. Being with you this season has shown me how much I was missing when I didn't have you in my life.

I like what I'm doing at ESPN. Sometimes I like it a lot. But I just need to find out if there's something out there that I could love.

I don't know if I'll get either one of these jobs. And if I do get one of them, I want you to know that I plan to come back. A lot. Or you could fly out to the West Coast and hang with me whenever it's convenient for you and your mom.

You have to trust me on how much I wish I could have been there for you today. But it's funny: As much as I've heard about me being there on the sideline and on the practice field for you this season, I always felt it was the other way around, that YOU were there for ME.

I guess I need to wrap up. And tell you at the end of this that it's official now that you turned out to be a much better son than I am a father.

Call you when I get there.

Your dad

THE EXTRA YARD

He didn't crumple it up when he finished, or throw it in the wastebasket. He just placed it on his desk and walked downstairs to the kitchen, where his mom was making them both sandwiches for a late lunch.

"So what did you think?" she said.

"At least this time he left a note," Teddy said.

She came over and sat down at the table across from him. "You okay?" she said.

"Are you planning on going anywhere?" he said.

"Only the store later. We're out of milk."

"Then, yeah," Teddy said to her. "I'm okay."

His dad called, as promised, right before they were getting ready to order in Chinese food for dinner.

"Hey," he said.

"Hey," Teddy said.

"Coach sent me a long text about the game," his dad said. "Congratulations."

"We played well."

"He said he even let you call the plays yourself at the very end."

"Yeah."

There was a long silence now, from both of them. Finally his dad said, "Did you read my e-mail?"

"Yeah."

"Did I do a decent job getting you to understand why I had to leave the way I did?"

Teddy said, "Does it matter?"

"To me it does."

"You gotta do what you gotta do."

Another silence, longer than the first one. This time Teddy was the one to end it.

"Listen, Dad, the bottom line is that I should have expected this," he said. "I should have known it was only a matter of time before you took off again."

"It's not like that."

"It's not?"

"You have to understand that this season meant more to me than I could ever possibly explain to you."

"Just not quite enough."

"That's not true, champ."

"Don't call me 'champ,'" Teddy said. "I've always hated it when you call me that."

"It's not true, *Teddy*. I'm still going to try to make it back for the championship game."

"Don't bother."

"C'mon, you don't mean that."

"I totally mean it," Teddy said. "I mean stuff I say even if you don't."

He took in some air, blew it out.

"You quit the team today," he said to his dad, and hung up.

THIRTY-FIVE

Teddy hadn't spoken to his dad since last Saturday night. He'd told his mom that if she heard from him, if he called or e-mailed her to let her know about what had happened with his exciting job opportunities, she should make it clear that he'd been serious about not wanting him to fly back for the championship game. She had promised she would.

As far as Teddy was concerned, his dad had moved on, and so had he. It turned out that a couple of months of being a full-time dad were all he had in him. Teddy explained all this to his friends: He was through talking about his dad. He just wanted to talk about beating the Norris Panthers and getting one step closer to MetLife Stadium.

Now, after a week of practice that felt like a blur, it was the night before the championship game against the Panthers, to be played the next afternoon at Holzman Field.

The Wildcats got home field because they had the better record. If they won tomorrow and stayed unbeaten, they'd also have home field the next week for the county championship.

If they won that, the next stop wasn't Holzman, it was MetLife Stadium.

Mrs. Madden had told Teddy to invite Jack and Cassie and Gus over for dinner. When they finished their burgers, and apple pie and ice cream, Jack asked if anybody wanted to play a little two-on-two football before it got too dark.

"I don't see how my mom playing would make the sides even," Teddy said.

"Hey," Alexis Madden said, "I've got moves you guys haven't seen yet."

"We don't need your mom," Jack said. "All due respect, Mrs. M."

"We've got three healthy players," Cassie said. "Who's the fourth?"

Jack smiled. "Me," he said. "I've been running. Doc says I can start throwing again."

"You can play?" Teddy said.

"Well, not tackle football," Jack said. "But I can do anything else. Including beat whichever two guys I'm playing tonight."

"No way!" Gus yelled. "Jack is back!"

"Back in the backyard, anyway," he said.

In their minds, Teddy's backyard would always mean the outfield at Walton Middle. Teddy ran upstairs, grabbed his ball off his bed, and the four of them then ran toward the field, Jack leading the way. It was, Teddy decided, the best possible way to get ready for tomorrow's game:

By trying to think about another game, at least for a little while.

The teams were Teddy and Gus against Jack and Cassie. Teddy told Jack it was only fair, as rusty as he was, to give him the best receiver.

"Great," Gus said. "I make you look like a real quarterback all season, and that's the thanks I get."

"I was just kidding," Teddy said.

"No," Cassie said, hands on hips. "You were most certainly not kidding."

They did play until dark, running around and complaining when one of the quarterbacks would take too long to throw the ball and then laughing even more. Jack and Cassie finally won when Cassie intercepted a ball Teddy badly underthrew, mostly because he wanted the game to be over.

Cassie, of course, treated it like the greatest defensive play since the Patriots' Malcolm Butler had picked off Russell Wilson to end that famous Patriots-Seahawks Super Bowl.

"I don't know if you guys are ready for tomorrow," Cassie said to Teddy and Gus as they walked back to the house. "But clearly, I am."

When his friends had gone home, Teddy went upstairs, got on his bed, and got out his playbook. Once more he was amazed at how thick it had gotten, how many plays his dad had added across the season.

He was looking at a couple of the last pass plays he'd added, one to Gus and one to Nate, when his mom came into his room and sat down at the end of his bed.

"I just want to tell you one thing before I turn in," she said.

"Please don't try to tell me that it doesn't really matter whether we win or lose tomorrow."

"Nope," she said, "not this football mom. No, sir."

She smiled. "I just wanted to tell you, once and for all, how proud I am of you, for the way you've handled everything this season, on and off the field. And what a great kid I think you are."

He smiled back at her, closing his playbook as he did. "Thanks, Mom."

"They wouldn't have made it to tomorrow with you," she said as she stood up. "I know enough about sports to know that."

He wasn't going to argue the point with her. In his heart, what he believed now was a great football heart, he believed she was right. He put down his playbook and walked over to her. He put his arms around her, and his head on her shoulder, the way he had when he was a lot smaller than he was now.

"I wouldn't have made it without *you*," he said.

They stood there for a long time, just the two of them, the way it had almost always been.

THIRTY-SIX

By ten thirty in the morning, two and a half hours before the championship game, Teddy couldn't wait any longer. He called Gus and told him to meet him at Holzman now.

"Jack's with me," Gus said. "On our way."

Teddy got into his uniform. He'd eaten a big breakfast at nine because his mom made him, even though he'd told her he wasn't that hungry. "You're not beating Norris on an empty stomach," she said. "Well, check that. You *could*. But I'd rather not risk it."

He took his ball with him when he got into the car. Even on the morning of the big game, you never wanted to show up at the field and not have a ball to throw around.

He got to Holzman first and saw that they'd put fresh chalk on all the lines. Somehow the town groundskeepers had made the grass look as good as new, as if they were starting the season all over again. They'd even written WILDCATS and PANTHERS in the end zones.

When Jack and Gus arrived, Teddy saw that Jack was wearing his number 12 jersey for the first time since he'd gotten hurt.

"You look good in that thing," Teddy said, "even without pads."

"I'd rather be in pads," Jack said, "and playing."

"I want to play right now," Gus said.

Teddy and Gus did their stretching. The three of them soft-tossed for a few minutes. When Teddy was ready to start throwing for real, Jack and Gus were his receivers. Teddy couldn't believe how good the ball felt in his hand, better than it ever had. Gus wasn't the only one who wanted to play right this minute.

Time seemed to go way too slow until noon, when it began to speed up the way it always did in the last hour before a game. The Norris team bus showed up, Scotty Hanley, their quarterback, leading them off it. There was another bus right behind it for Norris parents and family members.

The stands on both sides of the field began to fill up. Teddy heard them testing the public address system they'd be using at Holzman for the first time all season. Max Conte's dad, seated at a table under the scoreboard, was going to be the announcer. There was even a microphone stand set up in front of the Wildcats' bench; Katie Cummings would use it to sing the national anthem.

"This is all big-time today," Gus said, after Teddy had warmed him up along with the other receivers down near the goal line.

"Once the ball gets kicked off, it's still the same game we always play," Teddy said.

"You really believe that?" Gus said.

"Heck no!" Teddy said.

Somehow, as excited as they were and as nervous as they were and as impatient as they were for the game to start, they both managed to laugh.

Teddy waved to his mom when she got up to her lucky spot with Gus's and Jack's parents. There was nothing more to be said between them, because they'd said it all at home. Cassie and Katie arrived together. It was as if Cassie's last official act as Katie's coach was watching her sing the anthem.

Teddy walked over to say hi to them.

MIKE LUPICA

Cassie said, "The only thing that could possibly make today better was if I were playing too."

"Yes," Teddy said. "Having you in uniform would give us a *much* better chance to win!"

"Did I detect a note of sarcasm there?" Cassie said. "I certainly hope I didn't."

"Definitely not," Teddy said. "No, ma'am."

"For the last time, do *not* ma'am me."

She put out her fist then. Teddy gently pounded it. "Let's do this," said Cassie, the captain of the real home team in Walton.

Right before it was time for Katie to sing, Coach Gilbert walked the Wildcats down to their end zone, then told them to get in a circle around him and take a knee.

"I'll make this short," he said. "You know I'm not big at long speeches. But I just want you to appreciate the chance we've got today, and appreciate at the same time that win or lose, this will be one of those days we're all gonna remember. Just because you only get so many days like it in your life, and you can trust me on that."

He was making a slow circle as he spoke, as if trying to speak to each one of them directly.

"It's not just what we've done to get to today," he continued. "It's that we've made the journey together. You guys have picked each other up every time you had to, you've met every challenge, you've handled every test."

Teddy saw him smile.

"But now you are here. *We're* here. Together. And you know that today is no different from last week. If we win, we get another game. We get ourselves another one of these days." He paused and said, "And maybe another one after that."

Now Coach knelt down.

"Anybody here ready to stop playing yet?"

"NO!" they yelled.

"Are we gonna let those guys on the other side of the field stop us from getting to where we want to go?"

"NO!" They were even louder this time.

But Coach's voice was quiet when he spoke again. "Let's go make one more memory," he said.

He led them back to their bench. As they did, Teddy heard the screech of some brakes in the parking lot, heard the slam of a car door, and then saw his dad running toward Holzman Field.

THIRTY-SEVEN

It was one more thing, perhaps the last thing all day, that would happen in slow motion, especially since his dad was moving faster than Teddy had ever seen him, his old Walton cap on his head.

Teddy watched as he came around the bleachers, hopped the fence, and came right for him.

Teddy felt like running himself, but he knew there was no place for him to go.

"I told you not to come," Teddy said.

His dad was out of breath. His face was red. "Just hear me out."

"I did that already."

His dad put his hand on Teddy's arm. Teddy stared down at it, then back at him. But he let his dad walk him down the sideline about twenty yards, so they could talk in private. Teddy knew they didn't have long, because Katie was getting ready to sing the national anthem.

"Dad," he said, "the game's about to start. The biggest football game of my life. Even bigger than the one you missed last week."

"I almost missed this one too," his dad said. "They canceled the red-eye flight I was supposed to take from San Diego. I had to go through Chicago to get here in time."

Teddy was shaking his head again. "But I told you I didn't want you here."

"You don't always get to decide. I'm still the dad."

"Today?"

"Nah, kid. You're going to be stuck with me for a long time, I'm afraid."

"Why, because you didn't get one of those jobs?"

His dad smiled. "Actually," he said, "I got both of them."

"I—I don't get it."

"Turned 'em both down."

"But in your letter you said—"

"I know what I said about wanting to be happy, and doing something I love," he said. "But I finally figured out this week that you're the one who makes me happy. Being your dad is what I love to do most in the world. *That's* the only job I want."

He paused and said, "Okay?"

Teddy looked at him. Really looked at him. And saw him as clearly in that moment as he ever had. "Okay," he said.

His dad put his hands on both sides of Teddy's helmet and smiled again. *"Okay,"* he said.

They stayed right where they were while Katie Cummings sang a beautiful anthem. Then they walked back toward the Wildcats' bench together.

"How's the arm?" his dad said.

"Perfect," Teddy said, thinking that this was already a day to remember and they hadn't even tossed the coin yet.

"You really throw that block last week like Coach said?"

"I did."

"The kind of block I got hurt on, that kind of block?" his dad said. "Have I taught you nothing this season?"

"More than you think," Teddy said.

"Now you need to do one thing for me."

"What's that?"

"Play the game of your life."

Teddy did.

THIRTY-EIGHT

I t was 20–19, Norris, at halftime.

Teddy had thrown pretty much everything he had at the Panthers. His dad had thrown just about everything *he* had in his playbook. Teddy had completed one touchdown pass to Gus. Another had gone to Jake, when they'd completely fooled the Panthers on third-and-a-foot. Jake had snuck out of the backfield and gotten behind everybody, and Teddy had put the ball on the money for what became a sixty-yard score.

Teddy had also gotten his own six, on a one-yard sneak, lowering that shoulder again and feeling as if he were pushing back the whole Panthers line by himself.

But Scotty Hanley was treating this like a QB game of one-on-one, looking like even more of an undersized wizard than he had the first time they'd played him. He scrambled for first downs. He scrambled and threw on the run. He threw from the pocket, somehow seeing over the rush and finding open receivers. By halftime he had *three* touchdown passes.

"This is the best you've played yet," Teddy's dad said to him, the two of them at Teddy's favorite spot at the end of the bench. "It's all you ever hope for in sports, saving your best for the biggest game."

"But what if his best is better than mine?" Teddy said.

They both knew he was referring to Scotty Hanley.

"Well, kid, that's sports too, if that's the way it works out. But it won't."

"How can you be so sure?"

"Are you kidding? You think I came all this way for us to lose?"

The Wildcats were getting the ball to start the second half. Before the Panthers kicked off, Jack came over and stood with Teddy. So did Gus. And when Teddy turned around, almost as if he was supposed to in that moment, he saw Cassie on the other side of the fence, smiling at all of them, nodding her head.

"I'm just gonna tell you one thing," Jack said to Teddy, "and then I promise to shut up."

"Don't shut up!" Teddy said. "I need you."

"Just keep doing what you're doing," Jack said. "Don't force anything, and don't change a thing."

"Except one thing," Gus said. "This half we score more points than they do."

Before they took the field, Teddy's dad came over. "Guys have always told me, after they stopped playing, that nothing was as good as playing. I used to think the same way. But I was wrong."

"Lot of football left," Teddy said to him.

"Good!" his dad said.

Teddy threw his third touchdown pass of the game, to Mike O'Keeffe, on the Wildcats' second drive of the quarter. But Scotty matched that right before the quarter ended, breaking away from a Wildcats blitz and running twenty yards for the score. The Wildcats had missed their conversion after Mike's touchdown when Nate couldn't control the ball before going out of bounds. Scotty got his conversion, though, hitting his tight end.

Panthers 27, Wildcats 25.

One quarter left, unless somehow they ended up in over-time.

Both teams, after all the points they'd put up, after all the offense in the game, slowed down in the fourth quarter, exchanging punts twice. Scotty Hanley finally got the Panthers driving again. But with just over three minutes left, Max Conte caught up with him after another scramble and knocked the ball out of his hands from behind. Gregg Leonard recovered. Wildcats ball.

Teddy was standing between his dad and Coach Gilbert after Max's play. Coach turned to Teddy, grinning, and said, "You want to call your own plays the rest of the way, like you did last week?"

"Nah," Teddy said. "My dad's got this."

"We're gonna use short passes as runs," his dad said. "And then when they finally are expecting one more of those, we hit them down the field."

"And win this stinking game once and for all," Teddy said.

"Well, *yeah*," his dad said.

Teddy threw to Jake in the right flat. Then he hit Brian with the same play on the other side. First down. Two minutes and ten seconds left. He hit Gus on a neat curl, then made the same pass to Mike on the other side. Right, left. Right, left. He felt like a boxer throwing short punches. They were already at the

Panthers' thirty. Teddy threw a quick out to Gus on the right sideline for five yards, stopping the clock with a minute and thirty left.

Teddy looked over at his dad, who smiled and threw him a fist. Teddy put up his own fist, thinking, *Most fun I've ever had in my life.*

Jake brought in the next play. His dad was ready to take a bigger bite out of the Panthers' defense, a ten-yard shot to Nate over the middle. But before they broke the huddle, Teddy said to Gus, "If Nate's covered, I want you to take off."

"Roger that," Gus said.

Teddy shook his head. "You say some very odd things sometimes," he said.

"Copy that," Gus said.

The Panthers came with a blitz, and even though it didn't surprise Teddy, there was enough pressure to chase him out of the pocket to his right. He didn't even have time to check to see if Nate was open down the field; he was just trying to avoid a sack before he ran out of field.

He wasn't going to take a dumb chance. He remembered everything his dad had ever told him about quarterbacks eating the ball if they had to. But before he did that, he was going to do something else his dad talked about constantly:

He was going to try to make a play.

He reversed at the last second and began running to his left, back across the field.

As he did, he saw Gus Morales in the clear, behind everybody, waving for the ball as he ran toward the goalposts. Somehow Teddy was able to set himself just enough as he flung the ball across his body, and down the field, the best pass he'd ever thrown in his life.

He got hit as he threw but stayed on his feet, which was where he was when he saw the ball settle into Gus's arms in the end zone. That was right before Gus, the ball in his right hand, was raising his arms in the same moment the ref closest to him did the same thing.

Wildcats 31, Panthers 27.

Teddy calmed everybody down in the huddle, reminding them the game wasn't over. Brian brought in the play for the conversion: one more of his dad's naked bootlegs. Teddy could have run it all the way in, but he dove in just to make sure. They were up 32–27.

When he got to the sideline, his dad lifted him off his feet with a hug.

"I couldn't have made that throw," his dad said.

"I actually don't think I can make it either," Teddy said.

One minute left at Holzman.

THIRTY-NINE

Teddy watched that minute from his own forty-five yard line. He watched as Scotty threw a first-down pass deep down the middle to his favorite wide receiver, the play getting the Panthers to midfield right away.

His coach called their first time-out.

Scotty scrambled again on the next play, the Wildcats managing to put heavy pressure on him with just a three-man rush, everybody else dropping back into coverage. But when he got out of bounds, the ball was on the Wildcats' thirty-five yard line.

Forty seconds left.

On the next play Scotty crossed everybody up, running a simple, straight handoff to his halfback, who ran thirteen yards up the middle to the Wildcats' twenty-two.

Another time-out.

Thirty seconds left.

"I think the kid checked off and called that play himself at the line," Teddy's dad said. "Unbelievable."

"We just need a couple of stops," Teddy said.

"Somebody on defense has to make a play," his dad said.

Scott was forced to throw the ball away on the next play. Then he ran it again, all the way to the Wildcats' ten.

Fifteen seconds left.

Teddy couldn't breathe. And couldn't do anything. His game had become somebody else's game.

Scott rolled to his right now. He looked as if he might be able to run the ball all the way in. It was him against Andre Williams. Andre had to either come up on him or drop back into coverage. Do or die, truth or dare. Andre committed, and came up.

Trying to make a play.

As he did, Scotty Hanley stopped himself maybe a yard from

the line of scrimmage and threw this little floater to his wide-open tight end in the corner of the end zone.

Panthers 33, Wildcats 32.

That was the way it ended.

Teddy felt his knees buckle on the sideline, like he'd taken his last hit of the season. He even felt as if he might go down.

But he didn't.

Because then his dad's arms were around him, and not just keeping Teddy from falling to the ground. His dad was lifting Teddy up in the air, his embrace feeling stronger than it ever had, as if he never planned to let go.

They'd all gotten into the handshake line. The trophy presentation had been made at midfield. When that was over, Teddy sought out Scotty Hanley one last time.

"You got me good," he said, leaning in—leaning down, actually—and bumping shoulders with him.

"And you would have gotten me if you'd had more time."

"Some game," Teddy said.

He couldn't keep himself from smiling. Because it *had* been that kind of game.

"Best I ever played in," Scotty said, and then told Teddy he'd see him next year.

As Teddy walked away, it was sinking in that it was already next year for him, at least in football.

Coach gathered his players around him one more time and told them how proud he was of them, and that he was going to throw them the biggest pizza party Walton had ever seen next weekend. A few minutes later Cassie was on the field, telling Teddy and Jack and Gus that they were coming to her house for homemade pizza tonight.

It was an order, of course, not an invitation.

Teddy walked over and hugged his mom, as *she* told him how proud she was. Teddy thanked her. She asked if he wanted her to wait for him.

"Dad said he'd drop me," Teddy said.

"That was some entrance," she said, "wasn't it?"

"No," he said. "That was just Dad."

He walked back to where he'd left his helmet and his pads behind the bench. He'd put his jersey back on after he took off the pads, just because he knew when he took it off later, he'd be taking it off for good.

He saw his dad then, down the field, leaning against one of the goalposts, hands in his pockets, staring out at the field, almost like he was taking a picture of it for himself. For his own memory.

Teddy walked down there.

"I keep telling myself I should feel worse than I do," his dad said.

"Funny," Teddy said. "I keep telling myself the same thing."

"You know why I don't? Because I know you did everything you could. And I mean, *everything*."

"We both did," Teddy said. "That last drive of ours was perfect. The game just ended too soon."

"Like the season did."

Teddy shrugged and smiled again. "There's always next season," he said.

"There is that," his dad said.

He put his arm around Teddy's shoulders. They walked across the field to the Wildcats' bench then, both of them probably wondering how they could lose the big game the way they just had and still feel like they'd won so much.

A Reading Group Guide to
THE EXTRA YARD
By Mike Lupica

Discussion Questions

1. Where does the story take place? How important is the setting? If the author changed the town or state, how much would it affect the story?

2. Describe Teddy's character and how he changes during the novel. Talk about Teddy's fears and how he overcomes some of them. Jack says about Teddy: "I always thought there was a warrior waiting to break out." What does he mean?

3. Teddy reflects that, "If you thought of yourself in a certain way long enough—the way Teddy used to think of himself as the funny, out-of-shape loser—you finally just became that kid." Analyze his statement and discuss whether you agree with it. How does Danny's performance relate to Teddy's belief?

4. What is Teddy's relationship with his father like at the beginning of the story? Why is Teddy so angry with him? Discuss whether or not you think Teddy's anger is justified, and why.

5. Describe Teddy's father, including his strengths and weaknesses, referring to scenes in the story. Why wasn't he around when Teddy was growing up? Why has he returned?

6. Cassie gives Teddy advice about his father in Chapter 8. Reread her advice and discuss whether you think she's right. Does Teddy agree with her? Does he take her advice? If so, when?

7. How does Teddy's relationship with his father change? What is it like at the end of the book? Give specific examples of their interactions around football and outside of football.

8. Describe the visit to ESPN and the part it plays in Teddy's relationship with his father. Why is Cassie so interested in the visit and how does she react to it?

9. Teddy, his friends, and his mother are trying to save the music program at his school. Why is it threatened? What do they do to raise money? Discuss why they think the music program is important.

10. Describe parallels between competing in *The Voice* and competing in football. How does Teddy approach "coaching" in the singing competition and what does he learn from his experience?

11. Teddy's father saves the day at the music competition by handing a check to Teddy's mother in front of the audience. "Teddy wondered how she felt now that her moment had become his," meaning the father's. What does giving the check and the way he gives it show about Teddy's father? Describe the relationship between Teddy's mother and father, here and earlier.

12. Discuss Teddy's relationship with his mother. Would you consider her a good parent? What is her role in his sports life? How does she interact with Teddy's friends?

13. Talk about Jack and what he's like as a person. What adjectives would you use to describe him? How does he get injured and how does he react to having the injury?

14. What is Teddy's friendship with Jack like? What do they do for each other? Compare their characters, noting similarities and differences.

15. Use specific examples to describe Teddy's friendships with Cassie and Gus. How do the four friends interact as a group? Teddy says early on, "You keep score in sports, not in friendship." What does he mean and how does it apply to the four friends?

16. Describe Teddy's approach to football and specifically to being a quarterback. How does he prepare? Talk about ways in which he improves and why those improvements happen.

17. Jack says to Teddy, "There's more than one way to keep score in sports." What does he mean?

18. Jack likes to say you shouldn't "get ahead of yourself" in sports. What does he mean? What is Teddy's reaction to this idea? Does he succeed in not getting ahead of himself?

19. Coach Gilbert said to the team before the season started, "I want every one of you to make me proud this season. But more than that, I want you to make yourselves proud." Discuss whether or not Teddy makes the coach and himself proud.

20. When Teddy learns that his father isn't coming to one of the final games, his mother says to him, "Just control what *you* can control." What does she mean? Discuss whether Teddy succeeds in following her advice.

Guide written by Kathleen Odean, a former school librarian and Chair of the 2002 Newbery Award Committee. She gives professional development workshops on books for young people and is the author of Great Books for Girls *and* Great Books about Things Kids Love.

This guide has been provided by Simon & Schuster for classroom, library, and reading group use. It may be reproduced in its entirety or excerpted for these purposes.

Turn the page for a
sneak peek at the third book
in the **HOME TEAM** series
POINT GUARD.

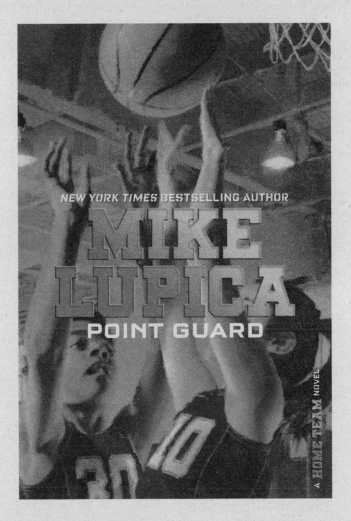

NEW YORK TIMES BESTSELLING AUTHOR

MIKE
LUPICA

POINT GUARD

A HOME TEAM NOVEL

This was how it happened sometimes:

You didn't want to stop, no matter how long you'd been playing.

That was the way Gus Morales felt right now in the gym at Walton Middle School, playing one last game of two-on-two with his best friends in the world.

It was Gus and Teddy Madden against Jack Callahan and Cassie Bennett. Jack and Cassie had won the first game. Gus and Teddy had won the second. Now the score was 10–10 in the third, game to eleven baskets, you had to win by two.

Gus had been feeling it from the start, making left-handed shots from all over the court even with Jack guarding him most of the time. And Jack Callahan could guard anybody, because Jack was one of those guys who took as much pride in his defense as he did in his offense.

But Jack wasn't the problem right now.

Cassie was.

She was suddenly matching Gus shot for shot, as if they were playing a game of H-O-R-S-E. Jack had carried their offense for much of the first two games, but not only had Cassie gotten hot, Teddy was getting tired chasing her. It was a bad combination for Gus and Teddy's team. No, check that. It was a *terrible* combination. And Jack was taking great pleasure in feeding Cassie the ball. He knew Gus Morales as well as anybody, and he knew that as much as Gus hated losing, he really hated losing to Cassie. In anything.

It was just pickup basketball, friends going against friends. It wasn't the league championship football game Gus and Teddy and the Walton Wildcats had lost the previous Saturday to the Norris Panthers. Jack hadn't been out there with them because he'd hurt his shoulder early in the season and hadn't been cleared to play sports again until today.

But this two-on-two game still felt like a championship after the way they'd been going at each other for an hour. Maybe it was just the championship of this one afternoon, and having the gym to themselves, which always made them feel like they'd won some kind of lottery. Maybe this was just one more occasion when they were playing for the championship of each other.

Everybody on the court wanted to win.

More importantly? Nobody wanted to lose.

Jack had just gotten a put-back after a rare Cassie miss to tie the game. They were playing winners out, which meant they kept the ball if they scored. Jack had it on the left side. Gus backed off, practically daring him to shoot. Usually that was a huge mistake, because when the games counted, you always wanted the ball in Jack Callahan's hands. But Gus could see that Jack was having too much fun being Cassie's assist man down the stretch to think about hoisting one up. It never changed, even as they went from sport to sport and season to season: the only stat that ever mattered to Jack was the final score.

Jack dribbled to his left now, stopped suddenly, then whipped a pass across the court to Cassie, who was to the right of the foul line.

"Teddy," she said as soon as she caught the ball, in a sing-song voice, "I'm coming for you."

"Leave me alone," Teddy said, giving her some room, hands on his knees and looking officially gassed.

"That is a big old no-can-do," she said. "It's you and me, big boy."

Teddy kept his eyes on Cassie but found enough energy to yell over to Gus and Jack, "Make the bad girl stop."

He was done, though. They all knew it. He had been trying to keep up with Cassie for three close games, finding out for himself what anyone who'd ever tried to cover Cassie already knew: chasing her was like chasing the wind. She was as fast dribbling the ball as she was without it. And she could shoot. Boy, could this girl shoot.

She could also chirp, the way she had just now, telling Teddy she was coming for him, calling him out one last time today, maybe even about to call her shot.

Gus wasn't much of a trash-talker. Neither was Jack. Neither was Teddy, as funny as he was. But all of Cassie's talk was just part of who she was, and they accepted it, mostly because she could back it all up.

She started her dribble with her right hand and took a hard, quick first step, as if she was about to drive past Teddy. But as soon as he bit on the move and backed up even more, Cassie stepped back. She created some very nice space for herself, and put up another set shot that seemed to float all the way up to the rafters before it finally came down, softly, through the net.

It was 11–10 for her team.

Still their ball.

This time, though, Cassie rushed her shot, trying to end things right here, and missed. Teddy got the rebound, threw the ball out to Gus.

They had a chance to tie.

Maybe it was going to take another hour for somebody to get ahead by two baskets.

Fine by Gus.

Jack came running out and got right up on Gus before Gus started his dribble.

"Gonna be like that, huh?" Gus said.

"Would you want it any other way?"

They both knew the answer. All four of them on the court knew. You couldn't be in this group and not throw everything you had at the other guy.

Or girl.

Gus decided to try a move he'd been practicing in his driveway. He was going to put the ball down with his left hand, as if he was the one who wanted to drive that way. But as soon as he did, he was going to whirl and go to the right. Using his right hand, his off hand, was something else he'd been working on as he got ready for basketball tryouts this Saturday. Might as well show it off now to the best defender in Walton.

Gus tried to sell Jack on the idea that he was going left again. Jack moved with him, overplaying, trying to cut him off. As soon as he did, Gus planted his right foot, spun around so he was facing the basket at the other end, and put the ball on his right hand, ready to cut to the middle, feeling Jack on his hip, knowing he had a step on him, at least.

As he did, he heard Teddy yell, "Gus!"

Too late.

Cassie had made her move as Gus made his, doubling him from behind, stealing the ball cleanly, turning defense into offense that fast.

She dribbled back out to the top of the key because that was the rule; you had to take it back there after any change of possession. As she did, Teddy pointed to Gus, telling him to take her, as Teddy moved over to guard Jack.

"Been wishing you'd make this switch all day," Cassie said, smiling.

"Didn't you ever hear the one about being careful what you wish for?" Gus said.

Cassie didn't answer. She was looking into his eyes, still smiling. As much as Gus was enjoying the moment, Cassie was clearly enjoying it more. This was exactly where she wanted to be. This was Cassie, 100 percent.

She dribbled with her right hand, then with her left, then her right again, as if she had the ball on some kind of string. Gus told himself not to watch the ball, to watch *her*, try to get a read on whether she was going to drive or pull back the way she just had on Teddy.

She decided to pass instead, off her last dribble with her right hand, her eyes never leaving Gus's.

Gus took his eyes off Cassie, though, just for a split second. He wanted to see where Jack was, how open he was, decide in another split second if Teddy needed help.

As soon as he did, Cassie broke for the basket, and the ball came right back to her: a perfect give-and-go. Gus scrambled to catch up, but now he was chasing her in vain the way Teddy had, watching as Cassie took Jack's bounce pass in stride and made the layup that won the game for their team.

Cassie stood underneath the basket, hands on hips, staring at Gus and looking like the happiest kid in Walton.

Gus said, "Is this the one where you tell us that girls rule and boys drool?"

"Never," she said. "I find that sort of trash talk *sooooo* uninteresting."

"On what planet?" Gus said.

Cassie laughed. So did he. Even now, he didn't want the day to be over. But it was all right, he told himself. The basketball season was just starting.

Gus Morales just had no way of knowing it wasn't going to be the season he expected.

Not even close.

From humble beginnings to billion-dollar sluggers,
this is the story of the New York Yankees—
the team of Babe Ruth, Joe DiMaggio, Derek Jeter,
and many more of baseball's all-time greatest.

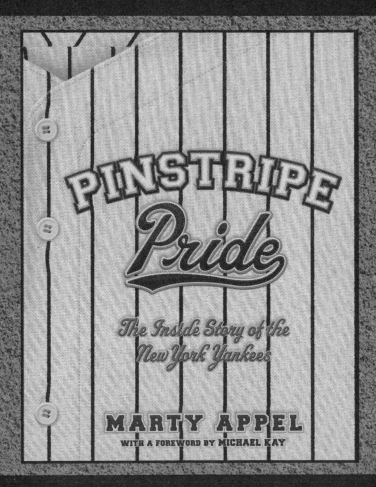

PINSTRIPE

Pride

The Inside Story of the
New York Yankees

MARTY APPEL

WITH A FOREWORD BY MICHAEL KAY

"If you love the Yankees, this is the book that takes you
backstage to see how they helped shape baseball history."
—John Sterling, Yankees broadcaster

PRINT AND EBOOK EDITIONS AVAILABLE
From Simon & Schuster Books for Young Readers
simonandschuster.com/kids

The journey of a lifetime brings surprises—
and maybe magic—at every turn.

From the critically acclaimed author
of *Nooks & Crannies* and *The Actual & Truthful
Adventures of Becky Thatcher*.

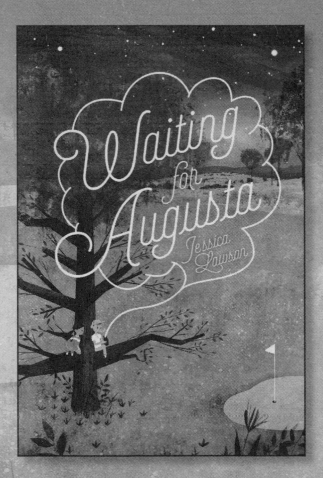

Six kids who don't get along.

Enforced exile in a public restroom.

A badly hidden childhood toy.

GARY PAULSEN

SIX KIDS
and a
STUFFED

(Cat) →

From this unlikely combination,
the unexpected happens:
They enter as strangers . . . and leave as friends.